SKYDIVING, SKINNY-DIPPING & OTHER WAYS TO ENJOY YOUR FAKE BOYFRIEND

SARAH ZOLTON ARTHUR

IRVING HOUSE PRESS

First Print Edition: October 2017

Irving House Press

P.O. Box 5738

Saginaw, MI. 48603

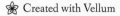 Created with Vellum

ONE

THE RISE

"I can't do it!" I yelled against the rushing of air, making it hard to hear myself, let alone hoping for anyone else to hear me. The roar was deafening, my eardrums ready to explode at this elevation.

"You sure?" asked my instructor, a sweet, pretty woman much braver than me. "I got you!" she yelled back.

For my answer, I pressed my body against the solid wall of the plane, opposite the open space.

"Whatever." The other instructor, Lennon, grumbled loudly and leapt out through the door with his client strapped to his body, on the count of three.

My instructor began to unstrap me, having her pinned between my tensed body and the cold metal wall, because how the other instructor and his client jumped, that was supposed to be how Lacy and I jumped before I chickened out yet again.

The fourth time I'd paid to jump out of a plane. Zero times completed. Zero. Zip. Zilch.

Once unhooked, and with the door shut, Lacy, able to

talk quieter now, patted my arm. "It's okay. We'll get 'em next time."

I hated disappointing Lacy. And she didn't have to tell me of her disappointment, no—the look on her face said it all. The same look she wore after failed jumps two and three as well.

Apparently, not after jump one. She'd been used to people backing out on the first attempt. But I owned a special kind of cowardice. The outright humiliating kind. The kind that so stunted your life you felt like other people could pick up on it from just a glance. Average height, cute outfit, coward.

Exactly as Brian had insinuated, well, it would be a year ago, now. A nice restaurant, wine, a beautiful night. I thought with the stage set, he'd been ready to propose. Instead, he'd crushed my future plans by breaking up with me. He'd been kind about it. At least, as kind as he could be under the circumstances. In his words, I'd grown boring. Set in my rituals. And he'd been right. I used to be a braver girl when we'd gotten together. I mean, I'd never been an adrenaline junkie or anything as extreme as that. Still, he knew the day it all stopped.

Brian had been nice, and in the beginning, he'd tried to help me move on. But I'd become stunted. He'd said he had dreams of adventures the two of us would share together, but after two years, he realized that dream was never going to come true. So he had to change his dream. And although he still loved me, that new dream didn't include me.

Like an idiot, I held on to the hope that he'd change his mind, that his leaving was a chance for me to get my act together so we could continue on with our lives, but maybe I'd be able to get some of that old Kami back.

Yeah, I held on to that hope until his facepage status

update told his friends, which at least online I'd still been considered, that he'd sold off everything he could sell, turned in the keys to his apartment, and bought his ticket to Argentina. Brian had pretty much fallen off the social media radar after that, too busy backpacking across a country. As his ex, I no longer rated an email or phone call which sucked, because I still wanted to know how his travels were going.

I heard from mutual friends, who did rate that call or email and felt like it had been long enough since our breakup to discuss Brian with me again, that he was happy. Met a girl from New Zealand not long after he landed, and they'd been adventuring together ever since.

Once I heard about him leaving, I decided to try to regain my bravery. It took me until six weeks ago, when I heard about New Zealand girl, to actually act on said decision. Every pay period I plunked down my three hundred dollars determined that this would be the day.

And I could post my video online for our mutual friends to tell Brian about. So he could see that if he'd only stuck it out a little longer...

Not today.

The plane glided along the runway, breaking. Lacy pulled the door open and stood aside for me to hop out once we'd come to a complete stop. Before I left, I turned to her. "See you in two weeks?" I offered.

"Kami, I feel bad about taking your money. I think maybe we should part ways."

"No. I got this."

"I don't think you do. I'm sorry."

So even my diving instructor broke up with me.

Great. Just great.

She took off walking toward the office and I followed a

little slower to collect my purse and phone locked in one of the ten guest lockers. We branched off inside the building as she headed to restock the gear, and I stopped in front of the row of lockers to press my temporary code in to retrieve my belongings.

My phone had been blowing up.

Messages. Messages. So many messages alerted me this friend or that friend posted on another friend's facepage. And they all said essentially the same thing: *Congratulations, Brian and Kiki.* Of course there were variations with more or less information.

Times like these, I wished we didn't share the same friends.

I walked back to my car, opened the door to a what could only be considered a sweatbox instead of a front seat, and immediately started the air conditioner to cool it down. Being up in the sky kept me cool, all that wind blowing and high-altitude chill. Back down here on the ground, the weather app on my phone said we were hitting almost ninety. But I refused to complain because it wouldn't be too long before all this glorious sun became a long, Michigan winter.

With the cool air blowing on me from the vent, I decided to torture myself a bit further and see what kind of ring he'd bought her.

No, I wasn't proud to admit that when I found out about New Zealand Kiki, I'd done some internet stalking, and her instaphoto page she'd left open to the public. I pressed the app button, waiting for it to load completely. Then I typed in her name. The first picture to load was a picture of her outstretched left hand sporting a giant teardrop diamond.

Very pretty. I always knew Brian would have good taste.

Not sure of the protocol here, did I leave a comment of congratulations to show no hard feelings? She'd written a caption beneath the picture: *One and a half years together and he finally proposed.*

Wait. That could not be right.

He'd only known her for a little less than a year. A year and a half ago, he'd still been with me.

Confused, I scrolled down to read some of the comments. One of them from Deirdre, a girl I considered a close friend: *Congratulations, Kiki! I know it had to be hard to wait for him to dump crazy Kami, but it was worth the wait.*

Dump crazy Kami?

So it wasn't a typo. They'd really been together a year and a half.

The rapid blinking, which usually worked to stave off unwanted tears, helped not one bit. Tears rimmed my eyes and began to spill faster than I could wipe them away.

There, feeling more stupid than hurt, I sat sobbing my eyes out like a total loser as the parking lot emptied around me.

"I need a drink." Only the empty car heard me lamenting on how my whole life had been a lie. How many other friends knew about Brian cheating?

At a time like this, it would've been nice to have tiny windshield wipers for my eyes as I backed out of my spot.

On the street, just past the airfield, I almost passed the turn into an old dive bar. The sign read Smokey's. It looked grimy and sad. Exactly what I needed to get through the rest of the day because I couldn't handle happy drunks. Not now. I needed people who had given up on life. People who the brightest part of their day came at the bottom of a whiskey bottle.

Slamming on the brakes, I made a quick turn into the lot, found a space, and shut the car off. Only four other cars and two bikes sat parked in the lot with me.

When I walked in, heads tilted up momentarily, eyes squinted at me, then those same heads dropped back to their glasses.

The grimy exterior perfectly matched the grubby atmosphere inside, along with the one waitress working. She looked as haggard as the outside of the building. Overly skinny, but not toned, she approached my table and stood there with her hip cocked, not speaking a word to me.

Apparently, the half a minute I took to decide on my drink was a half a minute too long for her. "Come on, blondie. I don't got all day." She griped in a voice of pure gravel. I looked up to give her my order, noticing she missed both of her top and one of her bottom front teeth. The hand holding two empty glasses from a neighboring table had yellowed fingers. Obviously, her dominant hand, the one she held her cigarettes with.

Her unnatural dye job needed a touchup. At least an inch of gray roots showed. That color red didn't fit her skin tone. Since I worked as a stylist, I felt pretty confident in my assessment.

"Gin and tonic," I ordered.

Now, I didn't particularly care for the taste of gin, but I remembered being told that it would get you drunk pretty quickly, and I desperately needed dunk and quick.

Before she left, I amended my order. "Make it two."

It wasn't but a minute later when she came back with my two gin and tonics. I slammed the first one like I'd slammed back a shot to get the alcohol infused into my system as fast as possible.

I needed not to feel. What I didn't need was for the

other skydive instructor to pull out the chair next to mine and plop down into it.

Not for the first time, I noticed how incredibly handsome he looked both in and out of a jumpsuit. More than hot, although he had that going for him too. Thick, brown, wavy hair just long enough to run fingers through and enjoy it. Crystal blue eyes. Depthless crystal blue eyes a girl could spend her life gazing into, a strong square jaw and a dimple peeking out from the corner of his cocky smirk. Not to mention his killer 'I jump out of airplanes for a living' body. Though I felt kind of meh about that. Brian had the same kind of killer bod, and look where that got me.

"Done staring?" he asked—no, that wasn't right. He mused, as if any part of him being here tonight of all nights could possibly be construed as funny.

"Pardon?" I did ask, jolted out of my hot guy trance.

"Heard Lacy dumped you."

Clearly, he'd sat down to be a donkey's butt. Yes, I'd been a coward once again. Didn't mean he had to rub my face in it. Which meant in lieu of answering, I sipped on my drink, wearing my most rueful face. But only partly due to his presence. The other part because I really detested the taste of gin. No matter. He didn't take my rueful face as the unspoken request I meant it to be—to go away.

"Appears she has a conscience. I don't have that problem and would be more than happy to be your new jump instructor." He used air quotes when he said "jump instructor." Then he took a drink of what smelled strongly of whiskey. "We can even meet here, eliminate the pilot fee." He snickered into his glass.

"No one invited you to sit, so you can go at any time."

Right then my phone took the opportunity to ping with a text from Deirdre, the girl I thought was my friend.

Hey, Kam. Got some news, think you need to hear.

The traitor. Why in the world would she text me? Just to get her jollies? Rub it in crazy Kami's face and report back to New Zealand Kiki?

So much betrayal swirling around, those darn tears started falling again—and in front of that donkey's butt to boot.

Ugh, I should've stayed in bed this morning.

"I can't do this." I admitted my feelings, slammed back the last of my drink, swiped my phone from the table, and pushed back my chair to stand.

The tears rolled harder now. A downpour.

"What the hell did that text say?" he asked.

"Nothing. Never mind. I'm a coward, a loser. We all know, the whole fricking world knows. I'm a coward and a loser. Don't worry. You won't see me again."

"Hey. *Stop*." He shot his hand out to catch my wrist, holding tight, despite me pulling hard at his hand to get him to release me. "*Kami. Stop*."

For some reason hearing him use my name made me not only stop trying to loosen his hold, but sit back down in my seat, too. I didn't even know he'd learned my name.

"What'd the text say?" he asked again. Too stunned to answer, I pushed my phone at him to read.

"That's not so bad... unless... you already know what she wants to tell you, don't you?"

I nodded.

"But it's worse than that." Then, to this virtual stranger, I launched into my tale of woe, from the breakup with Brian to finding Deirdre's comment.

He looked understanding, enough that I let my guard down. Today, of all days, I should have known better than to let my guard down.

The rat grabbed my phone and texted her back.

From my phone: *I already know. He's a cheater. You're a traitor and I couldn't give two shites about either of you.*

My first thought was he even made it sound as if I'd sent the text, avoiding the swears. I typically tried not to swear. Everyone who knew me knew I didn't like the swears. But that only lasted a moment, because then I remembered to be mortified.

"What are you doing?" I screamed, straining to snatch my phone back. He, of course, being larger, broader of shoulder, with a wider arm span, kept me from reaching it.

To my surprise, she came back right away: *Kami, I don't know what you're talking about.*

To which he replied: *Listen, my boyfriend is here. I have to go.*

Too late, because it happened *after* he hit *send*, I managed to snag the phone back.

"What are you doing?" I repeated myself, hissing instead of screaming. I was livid and clearly the screaming did no good. "I *don't have* a boyfriend. We know too many of the same people. Now she's going to see me as not just a coward loser, but a desperate, lying coward loser." The last part wasn't hissed because once the reality sunk in, my sadness and embarrassment replaced my anger.

He folded his hand over mine. "Listen, I have a month before I have to leave. I'll pretend to be your boyfriend. We'll take some pictures. You can post them."

"It won't work. Deirdre lives in town. She sees your face, she'll remember it. What happens when she sees you out cavorting with other women? It would make me even more pathetic than I am now."

"It's only a month. I just won't date anyone until I have to leave."

"You make it sound so simple."

"It is simple, Kami. I got you into this mess. Let me help you out of it."

"Why do you care?"

"Because I'm not the jackass you think I am."

"I don't think—" I started. He gave me *The Look*. That would be, the no-bullcrap look. "No, you're right. I've pretty much thought of you as a donkey's butt since the first day I showed up to jump."

The funny thing was he laughed and didn't look at all offended.

Deirdre predictably texted back: *Boyfriend? What boyfriend?*

"Ready?" my new fake boyfriend asked. "Our first official selfie as a couple."

Before I even had the chance to check for puffy eyes or fix my hair, he tugged my chair closer to his, draped his arm around my shoulder, angled his body to achieve maximum torso contact as he leaned his head in to look more intimate than friendly, and used his other hand to take our picture with my phone.

"Wow, I'm quite the photographer," he said, then flipped the phone around for me to see, laughing outright at my reaction.

Because my eyes, in fact, looked puffy, although my hair looked okay. He typed in the caption: *Len bought me skydiving lessons to help me get over my fears.*

He sent it. Then he powered off my phone and handed it back.

"Why'd you shut it off?" My mind still tried to reconcile the total one-eighty he'd pulled from the man who'd sat down maybe fifteen minutes ago to the man sitting there now.

Len shrugged. "She's going to have a lot of questions, which it'll kill you to ignore. Out of sight, out of mind."

"What do you know about my fears?"

"Nothing, but what you've said, what I've observed. The ex said you were boring, wouldn't go on adventures, and you've tried four different times to dive but backed out. Not to mention, you keep calling yourself a coward. Doesn't take a genius."

Well, since he'd been so forthcoming with his other answers, I decided to ask a more personal question. One that a girlfriend would know, one that I'd wondered about since I'd first met him six weeks ago. "Why Lenin? Was your mom a fan of the Bolsheviks?"

He'd been laughing at me here and there since first sitting down at my table, so this one shouldn't have affected me any differently, but as it sounded totally different from the others, it did. A deep, rumbling laugh sounding like it rose up from the pit of his belly. "Lennon, not Lenin. My mother was and remains a fan of The Beatles."

"It's nice. A strong, handsome name. It fits you."

"Why, Kami, did you just pay me a compliment?"

"Seemed like the girlfriend thing to do, if we want to be convincing. Where are you going at the end of the month?"

"Iceland."

"*Iceland?*"

He nodded. "My clients have a destination wedding to attend. Aside from the skydiving, I work on an eighteenth-century replica schooner cruise ship. Rich folk pay big bucks for the experience."

"Wow... you are pretty much my antithesis, with your jumping out of planes and big water cruising."

"I climb mountains, too."

"Why am I not surprised?"

"What about you, girlfriend? Where do you work?"

"Oh, I'm a hairdresser at Affinity Salon."

"That's the expensive place uptown, right?" Lennon took another sip of his drink, watching as I shook my head *yes*, as if my answer held the secrets to the universe. Though his reaction was far less intense. "Impressive."

Not compared to skydiving, schooner cruising, and mountain climbing, but I enjoyed the work and told him as much.

TWO

I woke up on Lennon's couch, well into the next morning, after he'd plied me with more gin and tonics yesterday, so I wasn't allowed to drive myself home.

That was my last memory.

The only reason I knew I woke on Lennon's couch was because it wasn't my couch and pictures of him with various people hung in frames on the walls around the room.

Somehow, I'd lost my pants during the night and my mouth tasted like unwashed butt.

And as I sat up, way too fast for the amount of alcohol I'd consumed last night, my head might have literally split open from my forehead to the base of my skull. At least it felt that way.

Shifting my feet to the floor, I rested my elbows to my knees, head in my hands, palms pressed to my eyes. Most times adding exterior pressure to counteract the internal pressure helped. Today it didn't help.

Luckily, my stomach felt fine. A fact I was even more thankful for when I saw the ibuprofen and full bottle of water sitting on the coffee table across from where my head had laid.

I unscrewed the cap, took a long swig, and downed the pills. Then because I heard rustling around in the kitchen, I stood up. My blood pressure dropped suddenly, probably from my massive headache. I got dizzy and fell back, my bottom to the cushion again.

Hand to forehead, I tried to shake away the dizzy spell and stood once more, this time much slower, and managed to stay upright.

The T-shirt I had on, not the one I'd worn to the jump yesterday, fell to skim my thighs just below my bottom and crotch area. My lack of clothing had me feeling a bit exposed, but when I looked (slowly again, not wanting to chance another dizzy spell) around the room to locate them, it appeared my pants had up and walked away.

Okay, so he'd seen my undies? I could hide out here for no real reason. I mean, I put on a fresh pair every day. Or I could follow the smell of bacon and maple syrup wafting from the direction of the kitchen. I followed the bacon. Because everyone knew unless you physically couldn't keep food down, bacon was really the only way to ease the stress of a hangover.

Lennon stood at the stove finishing the smoky, salty, meaty goodness. Puffy silver dollar pancakes topped with eggs and cheese waited for the bacon.

"Mornin', glory." He greeted me, using a spatula to expertly flip the perfectly crisped bacon onto a plate lined with a paper towel to drain.

This surprised me. The man didn't much look like he spent any amount of time in the bacon section of the super market, unless you counted that ultra-low-fat turkey "bacon." And let's face it, *ugh!* No one counted turkey bacon.

I groaned. "You're far too chipper for this time of morning."

Then he laughed that beautiful laugh at me again. "It's almost eleven."

"My point."

Finally looking up at me, Lennon jutted his chin in the direction of my water bottle. "Drink up. You don't finish, you don't get fed. And this is one of the breakfasts I've perfected. Trust me. You want this."

Challenge accepted, seeing as my head hurt too much to argue. I lifted the bottle to my mouth and sucked down the entire rest of the water without coming up for air. I sucked so hard, the sides of the bottle collapsed in on themselves.

"Jesus," he whispered. I looked up in time to see him swallow hard. What I saw in his eyes, well, I couldn't describe it exactly. Except to say he looked surprised, dare I say, a *good* surprised.

Though I thought it safer to avoid his look and comment altogether. "Feed me," I ordered.

He stared at my mouth one beat, two beats, three beats more before he honestly jolted, then began to finish the assembly of our—what turned out to be—pancake breakfast sandwiches and walked them out to the dining table.

I followed and sat at the place he left open for me. At the first bite, I could have sung *hallelujah*. When he'd said he could make them well, the man hadn't been exaggerating.

Still chewing because I was that classy and don't forget, *hungover*, I asked, "Where'd my pants go?"

Sandwich aside, he actually swallowed his bite before

he answered. "Wondered how long it would take you to ask. Your clothes are in the dryer. They should be done by now. Last night at the bar—"

"Did I puke?" I cut him off. Again, because I was a class act.

"Um... no." A smirk played at the corners of his mouth. He wanted to laugh at whatever picture, memory, danced through his head. Good choice not to laugh because I had my fist balled to punch him. Delicious food or not, hungover me was not as friendly as she could be. Or in this case, should be, as Lennon just kept surprising me. He wasn't the arrogant, impatient jump instructor I'd first met weeks ago.

"Then what'd I do?" I demanded snidely.

"You turned a mud slick into a slip-n-slide."

"I did *what*?"

He shrugged, as if drunk women did this in his company all the time. "There was a sloping mud slick, runoff from the bar's gutters. We'd just had all that rain. You saw it, shouted, 'I'm not boring' and belly-flopped onto the mud. You did it like four times before I could stop you."

"Four times?"

"You couldn't get in my truck covered in mud, so I had to strip you down in the parking lot." Before I could screech my mortification at him, he held up his hands, patting the air in that placating "hold on a minute" way people try to do to calm down a crazy person. "Nobody else was around. I made sure of it. And the parking lot was dark."

"How'd you get me into your apartment?" The crazy was leaving me, replaced by a healthy dose of shame.

"I pulled my T-shirt off and slipped it on you before we got out. So you were covered. Between my board shorts and you in the tee, which looked like a cover-up, if anyone saw us, they'd have assumed we'd been swimming."

It was at that moment something began to unfurl in the pit of my belly. Something not good—because it was *very* good. I recognized that something in the pit of my belly. A big, screaming crush. Yes, I had a screaming crush on the guy. In one night he'd managed to go from arrogant donkey's butt to this... this awesome representative of the male persuasion. I couldn't let him be my pretend boyfriend anymore, not with a screaming crush. I knew myself; it would get real awkward to the point he'd become super uncomfortable.

I knew it would happen because it happened once before, and not with Brian. What Brian and I had developed over time. I hadn't even been particularly attracted to him when he'd asked me out, but knew how hard it could be to summon up the courage to put yourself out there. So, what the heck, right? And I'd said sure.

No, the guy I'd gotten the screaming crush on happened to be my brother's best friend, Harrison. He was beautiful, had these crystal blue eyes, similar to Lennon's. But five years my senior, he wouldn't have anything to do with my sixteen-year-old self. Still, because my brother and I were close, they tried their best to include me until my stupid crush culminated with me making a pass at Harrison.

We'd been in the backyard of the house my brother and Harrison rented. It was located on a large property on the outskirts of town. They liked to ride four wheelers and snow mobiles, so the place made sense.

I'd thought we were alone outside at the bonfire we'd thrown to welcome Harrison's brother, Leo, for the summer. Leo was a year older than me and lived with his mother— their parents were divorced—in a different city so he could go to some smart school. We were waiting for him to arrive before commencing with the festivities.

Yeah, we weren't alone. My brother and Leo appeared from the shadows through the side gate of the house just in time to witness the humiliation of Harrison shoving me off his lips after I'd surprise attack-kissed him. I barely glimpsed either my brother or Leo but saw enough of them to know they'd seen all of my idiotic interaction. And heard Harrison go on to tell me that even if I weren't his best friend's sister, I was just a kid and he didn't get off on kids.

He wasn't mean when he'd said it, although his rejection sliced over every inch of me as if he'd fended me off with a butcher knife instead of the truth. His words stung like he'd poured lemon juice over those exposed cuts, because although not mean, he'd left no room for misunderstanding.

Right then, I packed up my stuff—purse, keys and jacket—and got the heck out of there, never to be in Harrison's presence ever again. It wasn't long after "the incident," as I'd come to call it, that he and my brother joined the Air Force together. And then it wasn't long after that that they decided to see if they had the stuff to become PJs. Pararescuers for the rest of us. Formerly known as parajumpers, hence the PJ, or the guys with medic training who fly into dangerous situations to extract the wounded, try to stabilize them midflight, usually under fire, and get them to hospital.

Neither Lennon nor I needed my crush to complicate the situation. Apparently, I'd been staring at him this whole time lost in thought, and I only became aware of my staring because he asked a playful yet defensive, *"What?"*

I blinked. "Huh?"

"Do I have something on my face?" he asked. Yes. A delicious smirk and dreamy blue eyes. The tiniest scar above his right eye, which gave a hint of ruggedness to his already-sexy model features. Though I couldn't exactly tell him all that.

"What? No."

"Then why are you staring?" This came with a corresponding chuckle, as if he read my thoughts. Could see into my mind.

"Quick, say something rude to me."

"I'm not going to say something rude to you. I like us getting along. You're... *fun*. Besides, a boyfriend wouldn't be rude. Consistency and all."

No, no, no. He had to be rude so I wouldn't like him any longer. The only way for him to be my fake boyfriend was for him to be rude to me. How could he not comprehend that, albeit without me actually explaining the situation, because um... no way.

And I think with the way he lifted that last bit of sandwich to his mouth, slowly biting, seductively chewing, he did it simply to annoy me. Okay, maybe he didn't purposely chew seductively. *Gah!* I threw my hands over my eyes and turned away. See? Awkward. Already.

He had to pick up on my awkwardness, yet he continued to disregard it. "So, here's what's on our itinerary today. We go skinny-dipping."

My eyes bugged. "Excuse me? We are not going skinny-dipping."

"We have to. I figure to work you up to the bigger challenges, like skydiving, we have to start off small. That's where you were going wrong. Starting too big."

"I'm not getting naked in front of you."

It was as if I hadn't even spoken. "Finish your food. Then you can shower and dress. After, we'll head down to the lake for some skinny-dipping. It'll be fun, liberating. You'll love it."

The first part of his plan, me finishing up my breakfast, I did without complaint. I was still intent to shut down any ideas about him and me skinny-dipping when I saw my phone sitting on his kitchen cupboard. I picked up my plate and walked over to the sink to load it into the dishwasher, powering back on my phone the moment I finished.

My phone pinged with several texts in succession. About five from Deirdre from last night, the others, though, came from our other mutual friends. It appeared Deirdre had been busy spreading the word about my relationship status. All of them wanting to know, *who was the guy?* I could deal with them. Until I got to the final text message. From Brian. What. The. Heck.

Brian: *He's going to help you overcome your fears?*

At least six months he'd cheated on me. What right did he have to even text, let alone leave a comment like that? I didn't owe him any explanation. *He* cheated. *He* left. *I* did neither. And standing in Lennon's kitchen, squeezing the life out of my stupid phone, I realized only one option remained open and viable to me. Or to us.

Lennon and I were going skinny-dipping.

THREE

"Turn around!" I yelled at the infuriating man as he stood waist-deep in lake water. Wet hair slicked back, droplets glistened off his olive skin, while he laughed like any of this was funny.

"I'm not turning around. And you're not a coward, remember? You aren't boring."

Well, I'd been trying not to be boring. But if the difference between being boring or not rested on whether I got naked on a beach in front of Mr. Super-Sexy, then maybe it could be good to stay boring.

My clothing he'd left folded and just-pulled-from-the-dryer warm on the closed toilet seat lid for the end of my shower, which had me thinking, this fake boyfriend stuff wasn't so bad. My real boyfriend never left warm-from-the-dryer, folded clothing for me. Although I'd done it for him plenty of times.

Then we left the apartment.

I begged him—down on my knees, hands clasped with fists full of his red cotton Nike T-shirt—*begged* him to stop off at my apartment to grab my swimsuit.

"No suits in skinny-dipping." That, and turning in the opposite direction from my home, was his answer.

"What about my car? I need my car. We can't just leave it at a bar," I said in protest and a healthy dose of fear.

"Taken care of. I have a friend who's bringing it back here. It'll be parked in my spot when we get back." Grr... he had an answer for everything.

Wait. The thought hit me, "I have the keys. How's he going to move my car without the keys? Hmm?" I smiled as I threw out that last indignant, hmm.

Yeah, I smiled too soon.

"He owns a flatbed," Len answered. Oh, I could see the smirk creeping over his lips as he stared straight ahead. The jerkface.

All hope was not lost. We passed a superstore. Superstores sold groceries, housewares, pharmaceuticals... and swimsuits.

"Please. It'll only take me a minute. I won't even try it on. Grab it. Buy it. Out."

"No suits in skinny-dipping." He repeated his earlier sentiment. Who said no swimsuits? He couldn't be the absolute authority on skinny-dipping.

It took us another half an hour to drive to the lake he wanted to take me to, one private enough to go *au naturel* and not scar small children for life.

And he'd been right to pick this spot. We had to drive down a path barely wide enough for his truck, a winding path through a dense wooded lot, which opened to a secluded lake with a small beach area. The beach, made up of large, pebbly, sandy soil, lacked the same invitation of its oceanfront counterparts. But the pebbles didn't seem to slow Lennon down in the least, peeling off the layers until he had nothing left to peel.

The man had no shame or modesty. He dropped trou right at the edge of the lake, showing off his *ass*ets (it's not a swear if it's part of the word) to the world, which in the moment consisted of me and the trees, as he waded into the water.

"Please. I'll take everything off. Just do this one favor for me," I begged.

"Depends on the favor."

Because I knew, just knew, I didn't have it in me to perform a striptease in front of that man, I gave it to him. "Turn around?"

He must have seen the true heart-stopping, vomit-inducing fear on my face, heard that same scared sincerity in my words, because Lennon actually relented.

"Fine. But it all comes off, Kam."

"I know. It will."

I watched him turn around and to his credit, not once did he look over his shoulder as I disrobed. First to come off were my tee and jeans. Next, slowly, one at a time in order to push back the inevitable, I toed off each shoe. I chose to hold onto my dignity a bit longer, making my way down the beach still in my bra and panties until I reached the water's edge. Then with no reason to put it off any longer, I stripped down to my birthday suit as promised. Definitely not the suit I wanted to wear.

Brian's text, however, came to my mind, giving me the courage to wade into the water.

So there you go, Brian. Along with Lennon's patience and encouragement, your ridiculous, totally uncalled-for response to my pretend happiness gave me the courage to strip bare and swim.

Cold. I shivered and wrapped my arms over my chest as I waded closer to Len. Being so much taller than me, his waist height equaled out to covering just below my breasts.

"Can I turn back now?" he asked.

"Yes. Thank you—*oh my god!*" I shrieked, leaping onto Lennon, where he had no choice but to wrap his arms around me to hold me up. "I think a fish just tried to get to know me biblically."

"Thank you, fish," he mumbled. And to my horror, I realized I'd plastered my naked chest against his nakedness, and let me just say how good all that satiny skin and muscle felt pressed against me, one of his hands holding onto my naked bottom.

I tried to push out of his hold. He predictably held tighter but allowed me to slide down his body, which was almost worse because even wading in chilly water, I could feel a specific and highly impressive area of his anatomy. Highly, highly impressive. Enough for me to close my eyes and swallow hard while the jerk chuckled in my ear.

"You can let me go," I told him, with a bit of edge to my voice. A year I'd neglected my girl parts by avoiding those boy parts.

"I'm good," he replied, chuckling harder at the edge in my voice.

"Why do you want to torture me?"

"I'm not trying to torture you. Well, no, that's a lie. I might be enjoying this a little. Why is your heart beating so fast now, Kam? The hard part's over."

"No, no..." My response squeaked out. "The hard part you've got pressed against my belly."

I thought I'd get another laugh. What I got was Lennon's crystal blue eyes staring deeply into mine. "I'm going to kiss you now." He warned me as his head descended, tilted to the right.

"Okay," I whispered back, having fallen under his spell until it hit me, and I hit him with a palm literally to his chest. "You can't kiss me."

"Why not?"

"Because we're *naked*." And yes, I whispered the word *naked* as if someone else could hear me and not see our two unclothed bodies.

That got me the laugh I'd expected before. "Naked is the best time to kiss, fearless."

He called me fearless. And then he kissed me. Universes expanded in that kiss. Stars went supernova in that kiss. Civilizations rose and fell.

The closer he held me, the harder he pressed his lips to mine, exploring my mouth with his tongue, coaxing me to explore back. Nothing in my life had felt like it. No kiss I'd given or received made my heart feel on the brink of exploding. Soft and hard, powerful the way a good kiss should be.

Lennon moved one of his hands to grip my hair, positioning my head exactly where he wanted me, to deepen the kiss further.

I might have figured out the meaning to existence because of his lips.

"Well, all right!" yelled a distinctly male voice coming from behind us. So not Lennon's, obviously. "Got here just in time for the good stuff."

The good stuff? Jesus. I froze in his arms. To his credit, though, Len stopped his beautiful assault on my lips, whipped his head up to look at our intruder, and shoved me behind him, all without exposing any of my lady bits, in one smooth move.

"No, dude," the guy on the beach called out. "Don't stop on my account. Your lady is *hot*. Dudes like you always get the hottest chicks."

He sounded like a stoner. He sounded stoned. And even worse for me, he wasn't alone. Three other young men watched us from the beach in their rumpled jeans and T-shirts. Smoke billowed out of the open door to a nineteen seventies conversion van. Copper, with a Native American woman and a feather airbrushed where I would've wanted a window on the backend of the vehicle. And I thought I counted three more sets of feet sitting inside the van.

Oh, but that wouldn't be the worst part. Far from it. The worst part was noticing the stoner dude held a cell-phone in hand aimed at Lennon and me.

"Stay with me, fearless," Len ordered, moving through the water up toward the beach's sandy soil.

I didn't even give "stay with him" a second thought, plastering myself to his backside. One of my hands on his shoulder, the other he held tight and close, resting against his chest. Over his heart, if I was the kind of girl to notice, which I totally wasn't. Not at all. *Shoot.*

And the stoner kept right on filming us.

"Make him stop," I pleaded to Len. Big and bad*arsed*, he could do it.

"No," he told me. No? "I have a better idea." The water level dropped to around our knees, then calves, ankles until, with me still plastered to his back, Lennon stood on the beach in all his naked glory. "Toss me the lady's clothing, will you?"

"Dude, get the hot chick's clothes," Stoner-boy called to his friend standing closest to my jeans and tee. He walked them over to Len, who grabbed them and turned, to my mortification, to my utterly naked self.

"Arms up," Len ordered me. I put my arms up, not caring in the least the girls went unwrangled as he slid the shirt down, making it his mission to caress all of my curves as he did. Then I held on to his shoulders as he slipped first one leg and then the other over my feet. Yanking them up my wet body became a test of pure will. Man versus denim. In this case, thankfully, man won. Lastly, he helped me back into my cute little white canvas sneakers. Though, neither of us took the time to tie them.

Then he pecked the tip of my nose. Pecked my lips, and turned tail to collect his clothing scattered from the water's edge back to where we'd parked.

So yeah, I watched him the whole time he dressed. Not my proudest moment, but I had a screaming crush. And he kissed me. And shielded me. And he helped me dress. And he was much better at being a pretend boyfriend than most real boyfriends were at being a real boyfriend.

As Lennon made his approach to the stoner with the camera phone—I thought to take it and erase the evidence of him and me in the lake, naked together—he instead asked the guy, "Can you text that video to me? I want to post it to my Instagram."

You couldn't see anything more than my upper back and part of his chest and shoulders (at least while we'd been in the lake), but that wasn't the point. *I* knew I was naked and so had to assume the others would know, too.

"What?" I shrieked. The shriek he paid no attention to as he busied giving his number to the stoner.

Horrified, I watched the stoner upload the video into a text and a minute later, heard the ping on Lennon's phone that he'd received said text.

Len opened the text, pressed some buttons on his phone, then held his arm out to me. "Come here, fearless." Uh... no. That wasn't going to happen. Not with me contemplating between running off or killing him. "Kami. Come here, sweetheart."

Shoot! He called me sweetheart. That was new. God, he was so good at this fake boyfriend stuff. So good, my shoes stuck out their tongues at me and walked us over to him, despite my initial internal protest.

His arm snaked around my waist, Len held me tight. "He did us a favor. You need proof of your bravery or no one who knew you with your ex will believe this first adventure. Now you have proof."

Made sense. "Then Brian can kiss my butt."

"Then Brian can kiss your butt," he agreed. "But not literally. That's my job." And he said that with a wink, giving my waist a squeeze.

Realizing I hadn't friended Lennon on any of my social media accounts, I did that from my phone before uploading the video of us skinny-dipping that he forwarded to me.

And just because I could, I made us facepage official.

Immediately, my phone blew up with notifications from friends who commented or liked the video.

Truth be told, it kind of skeeved me out that so many people liked *almost* seeing my naked bum. Or maybe it had nothing to do with me. Fingers crossed, it was Len they admired so readily. Len had a body deserving admiration. Though the more time I spent with the guy, the more it became clear his insides deserved that same admiration.

"We're quite the sensation among my facepage friends," I told him while still looking down at my phone, yet managing to successfully open the passenger door to his truck and climb into the seat. Lennon shut the door for me. "I'd say that's a good start for bravery. What's on for tomorrow?" I had to inwardly chuckle at my diversionary tactic. Len didn't need to know my shift started early tomorrow. As far as he was concerned, I had all the time in the world.

In reality, the skinny-dipping did me in and I was ready to head home and hide from the world for the rest of the day.

I chuckled too soon.

"Tomorrow?" he asked, but I could tell it was more of a statement by his mischievous tone. "Oh, *silly*, *silly* girl. We aren't done with today."

Exactly as I feared. Me. In trouble. Again. My mouth dropped open for probably a half a minute of stunned silence. What was he trying to do to me? "We aren't?" I finally managed.

FOUR

The longer we rode in silence—and I'll admit to careful observation of Lennon, who appeared deep in thought, lips going from pursed to the bottom being tugged between his teeth—the more it became apparent that he had not one clue as to what our next adventure should be.

Yet he refused to let me go home.

Then without any warning, and the both of us in sticky, damp jeans, he yanked the steering wheel to the left to turn us down a road leading to the interstate.

"Where are we going?" I asked. "Are you trying to kill us?"

"I know our next adventure, and no. Hard to show up your ex if you're dead."

"Well?" I asked snidely, even to the point of folding my arms across my chest and tapping my foot against the floorboard.

In what I discovered to be true Lennon fashion, he asked back in far too chipper a tone. "Well what?"

My eyebrows raised in my best unspoken "don't bullcrap me." I released what I hoped would sound like a long, suffering breath. "Where are we going?"

"I guess you'll have to wait and see, ye of little faith."

Part of me wanted to laugh. Lennon, it seemed, could be adorably charming when he wanted to be. Which for me to say was saying something. Especially in the face of being forced to participate in another one of his ridiculous adventures.

My phone pinged so much from notifications of my friends liking or commenting on that darn video, I had to turn the notifications off.

When I didn't protest any longer about our next destination, he let me know how my acquiescence pleased him by reaching his hand over to squeeze my knee affectionately, then grasped and held my hand. Another very real boyfriend move for a fake boyfriend to make. And I secretly loved every touch. Big ol' screaming crush and all.

When he finally exited the interstate via the deserted off-ramp, to the left of us, trees and road. To the right, trees and road.

He turned right, which meant he had to have some idea of where we were headed. Up ahead I saw what looked to be the beginnings of a town carved out from the forest. But the closer we got, it looked more like a town in which the people had *started* to carve it out, found it too difficult, and abandoned the location.

"You brought me to a ghost town?" Not sure how I felt about this newest adventure.

"No." He laughed. "But that's a great idea to add to the list."

"Gee, thanks," I murmured.

He let go of my hand, lifted his to wipe away the line of sweat formed above his upper lip, and adjusted the air conditioning. Then he pointed to an old filling station that may or may not have still dispensed gasoline.

"Our next adventure is a gas station?" I asked incredulously. Because really, how else could one ask that sort of question?

"No, sweetheart, it's not the gas station we want—it's what's inside."

Len clicked on his blinker despite being the only car around for miles, then slowed and turned into the parking lot, proceeding behind the building where I was actually surprised to see several cars parked. And he pulled into a spot next to a black Chevy Silverado.

But before I got my door open, Len leaned over to me, pulling my head closer to him by my chin and dropped a quick, sweet kiss on my lips.

Really? What part of my screaming crush did he not pick up on? It felt as noticeable as the nose on my face. Just as fast, he released my chin and hopped out of the cab, leaving me sitting stunned again as he approached an old door that lacked the ability to close properly, leaving about an inch gap between the wood of the door and the frame.

When he turned back around to me, it was with a smirk firmly in place. Oh, he was so cruising for a punch to the gonads.

"You coming?" he asked, his voice full of cheek. And worse, the jerkface didn't even wait for me, pulling on the handle and proceeding inside.

I slid from the truck, running to catch up. Lennon wasted no time, already at the order window with his wallet out handing the girl on the other side a twenty-dollar bill.

"'Bout time," he teased. "Maybe find us a seat instead of standing there?"

Grr... cheeky cuteness—otherwise known as the *worst*

kind of cuteness because of it being the *best* kind of cuteness.

Nodding seemed the smartest course of action as I couldn't stop thinking about that kiss to begin with and him being all Lennon... Only bad could come from this crush. Very, very bad...

"Well?" he asked, using his eye roll to tell me to *get moving.*

His comment snapped me out of my dazed, incredibly ridiculous thoughts, but also accounted for the blush spreading over three-quarters of my body. I turned away quickly and scanned the room to avoid having to speak to him directly.

On the far wall opposite the restrooms I spied an empty table and made my way over to it. Out of the corner of my eye I noticed another person heading for the table too, but as I never looked his way, I could claim complete deniability if he chose to confront me about the table I reached first. And since Len's job in this scenario meant playing my boyfriend, fake or not, I was fairly certain he'd stick up for me in the event I needed to be sticked up—*stuck up*—for.

As it turned out, probably because dude got a look at Viking-thunder-god Len, he veered past our table trying for another about four spots down. Len curiously pulled the chair kitty-corner from mine instead of across from me and sat, his manspreading knee brushing the side of mine.

Was that heart palpitations or gas? *Please be gas... Please be gas...* His knee brushed mine again. *Shoot!* Not gas. Most definitely *not gas.* I took a deep breath and tried to steady myself before we both heard my voice quivers. "So?" Okay, good. Zero quivers. I had this. "Are you going to tell me the challenge?"

"Give it a sec."

The order girl, in her oversized yellow T-shirt with the sleeves rolled a couple of times so the short sleeves didn't hang too far down her arms and the words *Coop's Wings* printed on the front in large black lettering—walked over with a paper and pen in hand. She set the paper down in front of me and held the pen out waiting for me to take it.

I read the paper: *This is a challenge you have volunteered to partake in. The establishment holds no responsibility...*

At *'holds no responsibility,'* I realized I held a waver they wanted me to sign. A waver? For?

That was when a group of guys from another table stood to circle ours, shouting taunts of "no way" and "it's a lost cause," to single out a few.

What the ever-loving heck? They didn't know me. I still didn't know what I was signing for, but I scribbled my name across the bottom line, sealing my fate because the moment I set the pen down, the cook from the back placed a red, paper-lined plastic basket on the bar top and shouted, *"Order up."*

The waitress took the waver and pen with her when she left to retrieve the basket. I watched her open the fridge to pull out a gallon of milk. She poured a tall glass and set it on the tray next to the basket. Next came the celery sticks piled in a second paper-lined basket set on the tray, too.

Then she walked the whole tray over to our table.

In the first basket, chicken wings. No, not just chicken wings—the most vibrant red-sauced chicken wings probably in the history of sauced chicken wings. And I knew the challenge in an instant. More like *smelled* the challenge in an instant. The caustic, unforgettable aroma of capsaicin burned my eyes, singeing the fine hairs in my nose.

"Len, you've got to be kidding me," I said.

He smiled his devilish smile and laughed not a faint chuckle, but a full-bodied robust, throw-your-head-back belly laugh.

All the while the waitress configured the milk, celery, and wings in a semi-circle on the table around me, along with several packets of Wet-Naps.

I saw a guy on television do this once. *How hard could it be to*—Those backward-ballcap-wearing-frat-guys kept up the taunting making it hard for me to concentrate. I still had no idea if I'd actually go through with this idiocy. That sauce could burn a hole through my esophagus. Although, if I died, it would be with my clothes *on*.

Declining the challenge almost became a reality when I heard it, the words that triggered a desire to show up those jerkfaces in the biggest way possible: *She won't do it, she's just a girl.*

Just a girl?

Maybe I was a chicken, but that had *nothing* to do with me being a girl.

Choice made, I'd show them what girls were made of.

It took a minute of surveying the tablescape to figure out how I was going to go about this. Fast was the key. It would be my only chance to win this mother-trucker of a challenge. Once I had an idea in place, I went for it.

My stage one strategy: Open all six Wet-Naps packets, pull several regular napkins from a container on the table, and place them ergonomically as well.

"Okay." The waitress held her hand in the air, silencing the small crowd. "You have twenty minutes to finish these six wings. No getting up from the table. We provide you milk and celery to cool your mouth. If you need more, raise one hand. If you quit, gesture '*out*' like an umpire. When you finish, raise both hands in the air. Do you understand the rules?"

I sucked in a big breath. "Yes."

"What's your name?" she asked.

"Kami," Len answered, and I'd swear he sounded proud.

The frat boys surrounding our table began to chant, "Kami...Kami..."

Well that certainly was a change from a minute ago.

I locked eyes with the waitress, raised my eyebrows, and nodded.

She produced a phone from her pocket, pulled up a timer app, and dialed the numbers to twenty minutes. "Ready?" she asked. And without waiting for another verbal response, she shouted, "Time starts... *now.*" Then she hit the *start* button.

My second stage strategy: Pick up the first wing, pop the whole thing in my mouth, and scrape the meat off in one go. I gave a couple chews, then swallowed. Delayed reaction.

Oh heck, delayed reaction. This might almost be worth a swear.

My mouth ignited in pain. Unbelievable, burning pain. Snot ran down my nose, the tears in my eyes practically blinding me as I fumbled for the glass of milk, drinking the entire thing down without coming up for air. I threw one hand up to signal more milk.

Forget my mouth, my whole body burned from the hell-fire (that's not a swear, it's a thing) as I picked up the second wing, this time, knowing what to expect, I hesitated, not wanting to put myself through that unimaginable torture again. But knowing I had to.

The second wing went down with steel determination.

After a second glass of milk and two celery sticks, I picked up the third. It went down not from my steely will, but my sheer hatred of Lennon in that moment. Perspiration soaked my T-shirt and rolled down my brow. Even the best deodorant couldn't mask the capsaicin sweat stink.

I'd kill him if I made it out alive. Lennon had to die. Slow and painful. Like dig-a-hole-in-the-ground, shove-him-in, bury-him-up-to-his-neck-and-slather-his-head-with-honey-next-to-a-fireanthill painful.

In the background the frat boys still chanted, *"Kami... Kami..."*

Three left to go. Three. Could I do it? I couldn't do it. But I had to do it because of Brian and New Zealand Kiki. Because of Harrison and my brother. Because of me. I'd lost me. I knew the day, the place, the time I'd lost me. Now I needed to get me back.

Wing four went down with the aid of more celery. Wing five, my tears blinded my eyes to the point I couldn't see to grab the milk, almost knocking it over. Len grabbed it in time, wrapping my fingers around the glass. By the sixth wing, I thought I was going to puke. If I puked, I lost. I *would not* puke.

Last bite chewed and swallowed, I threw my hands in the air Rocky style and the waitress hit *stop* on the timer.

"You finished with six minutes left on the clock," she said.

I couldn't speak, but I smiled. The cook came out front with a Polaroid camera to take my picture, then handed me a T-shirt. Black with yellow lettering, *I Conquered Coop's* written on the back, Coop's small logo on the front. I held it for all of fifteen seconds, long enough to shove it at Len and run to the bathroom, pushing women out of my way to get there.

Let me just say, it burned every bit as bad coming back up.

Strong, gentle hands held my hair back until I finished. Len scooped me up into his arms to carry me out to the sink. He set me on the basin, washed my face and hands with soapy, wet paper towel and helped me change into my non-pukey new tee. We had to throw the other one out. There was no saving it. No saving it.

Dear lord, I shook from the force of my regurgitation. Lennon never left my side, although I had to walk out on my own or I'd never forgive myself, but he kept a hand around my waist.

"You did great, fearless," he whispered in my ear. A whisper that felt intimate and made me shiver, so I supposed it was good I'd been shaking to begin with or he'd know how he affected me. "Come on. Let's get you home."

Wholeheartedly, I agreed with that offer. I needed to go home, put on my comfies, snuggle on the couch with a thick blanket (I kept the air conditioner set to frostbite), and watch a movie until I passed out.

He helped me inside the truck, running—not walking—around to climb in on the driver's side.

The ride home stayed pretty uneventful, but the first problem occurred when he drove us in the opposite direction of my house. Having gone through this area earlier today, I knew without a shadow of doubt Len was taking me to *his home*.

What about my comfies? My blanket? My movie until I passed out? I mean, I hadn't actually expressed my desires yet—I could hardly speak. But how could he not pick up from my haggard appearance that I needed to rest? Not more of his silly challenges.

So on the heels of the first swooped in the second problem. That being I had not one ounce of gumption left in me to argue. The scoring heat from the wings and subsequent retching had done me in. Plus, he stopped at the grocery store just down the block from his condo, kissed my cheek before he ran in and less than fifteen minutes came back with two bags of ice cream—including the ice cream condiments—and a toothbrush, because he was just that sweet. Five minutes after that, he had us back at his condo.

This time, he helped me from the truck and wouldn't let me take even one bag.

If this was his pretend boyfriend, imagine him as a real boyfriend. *He's going to make some girl very lucky someday.*

The very first thing he did when we got inside was to set the groceries down on the bar and jack up the air the way I do it at my place.

He led me into his room, where he pulled a pair of drawstring pajama pants—black and yellow plaid to match my T-shirt—from an old maybe pine dresser that looked like he'd gotten it secondhand and handed them off to me before he dragged the comforter and both pillows from the bed as he left.

"Come out when you're done," he said.

Once the door closed on his phenomenally fine backside, I dropped trou and changed into the drawstring sleep pants, pulling the drawstring tight to cinch at my waist or those puppies risked falling around my feet otherwise. Len had even left the new toothbrush setting on the bedside table for me to see. With a heart full of gratefulness, I picked it up and walked into his bathroom.

My whole mouth got the scrub down; teeth, tongue, cheeks walls, gums. Lennon even used minty, whitening toothpaste—which meant *I* used minty, whitening toothpaste. Once my trash dump of a mouth tasted clean enough, and I felt confident I wouldn't kill Len with my toxic halitosis, I rejoined him in the living room.

Both pillows rested one on top of the other against the arm of the long, deep sofa. I sat down as directed, folding my legs under me.

He draped the blanket over me, even tucking it under my chin. Snuggly. "Be right back."

You'd think it would be awkward, me tucked like a little kid and not even a television on, but he made me feel so comfortable, it forced any residual awkwardness out.

After only a minute, he came back from his bedroom dressed similarly to me in drawstring jammies and a T-shirt. Instead of coming to me, he walked into the kitchen.

The sound of spoons clinking against glass or stoneware bowls drifted into the living room. Less than ten minutes more he walked back out with a tray covered with two Fiestaware-esqe bowls filled to overflowing with ice cream, hot fudge, nuts, whipped cream, and even double maraschino cherries on top because everyone knows maraschino cherries are the best part of a hot fudge sundae. *Boom!* Mic drop.

"Hands up," he ordered. "Palms out."

Oh...kay. I followed directions, putting my hands up, palms out. He set the tray on my open hands before tuning to pick up the remote. He flipped the cover up, plopped down next to me, and flipped them back over the both of us. Still not taking the tray, I might add.

Although not heavy, my arms strained, not being used to holding anything in this way.

"Hello?" I said.

He glanced over but didn't answer.

"Uh, the tray?"

"You've got it." Rather than taking the tray, he turned

on the television, bringing up the guide, scrolling through the on-demand movies as if he had all the time in the world. Finding what he wanted, he pressed the *select* button and finally—*finally*—took the tray from me.

Lucky for him, I found out about his amazing sundae-making abilities or he might have been destroyed.

The title of the movie came up on screen and I felt like I couldn't breathe.

Jump Squad. A movie about pararescuers. After the day I'd had, I couldn't deal with this. Could. Not.

Len turned to say something to me. "Jesus, Kam. Breathe, sweetheart." I didn't think that was what he'd intended to say. He took my bowl and set it on the coffee table, immediately pulling me onto his lap. "What's wrong?"

"PJs," I managed to utter against his neck.

"What about them?"

"I can't. *My brother. Harrison...* They—*I can't.*" Then the waterworks started. Despite the crippling cowardice that kept my brother and his best friend to the forefront of my mind, I actually tried on a daily basis *not* to think about them by name, as this always ended up the result.

"Okay... okay. We'll watch something else." He quickly turned off the movie, opting instead for a Kristen Bell comedy. "You wanna talk about it?'

"No," I said, shaking my head *yes.*

He chuckled, but it sounded uncomfortable. "Give me something to work with, fearless."

"That's just it—I'm not fearless. I stopped being fearless a few years ago."

"I got that."

"No, you don't." I hiccupped. "My brother died. My

brother and his best friend, Harrison, died because I confused fearless with reckless."

He waited me out, waited for me to continue, squeezing my hip for reassurance.

"I had a crush on Harrison," I said.

Lennon's arms tensed around me.

"One night my stupid teenaged brain thought I should kiss him and maybe he'd want to go out with me. All it did was make him uncomfortable around me."

"So you had a crush. People have crushes."

Gah! He didn't get it. "Stop trying to make me feel better. My brother and Harrison joined the PJs to get away from me. Their helo crashed going in to rescue some badly-wounded soldiers who were on some secret mission. All five men on board died that day."

"That wasn't your fault."

"It was. Harrison joined to get away from me. My brother joined so Harrison wouldn't go alone. Even Leo, Harrison's brother, blamed me."

Lennon squeezed me again.

"He blamed me so much, he terrorized me online. I had to turn off all social media for over a year."

"I'm sure he was just hurting. When people hurt, they need someone to hurt worse than they do," he said.

"No, he told me if I didn't kill myself, then he'd kill me and make it look like suicide. I called the police. Then my tires got slashed weekly. And *'clients'* would complain about me at work, clients I never worked on. I'd get written up. He *set that up*. He brought others in. I never knew where the next threat would come from. Since it wasn't one person, I couldn't even take out a protection order."

"*Kami.*"

"So I moved, ending up here."

"It wasn't your fault. He was angry. Sad. It wasn't you. Sweetheart, you have to believe me on this."

I shook my head *no* this time.

"Nope." He tickled me, the jerkface, to get me to look at him. "Repeat after me."

"No," I said out loud and he tickled again.

"Come on, Kam. 'It's not my fault'—say it."

The tickling intensified, no fair. Resistance futile... resolve breaking... "Okay," I shouted. "It's not my fault."

"Again," he demanded, controlling those tickling fingers with such dexterity, I thought my side might literally split open.

"It's not my fault," I shouted, even as I laughed and wriggled uncontrollably to try and get away. "Now stop."

"You done being so hard on yourself?"

"Yes." That came out loud enough for his neighbors to hear.

His fingers abruptly stopped the tickle assault and he kissed my nose, scooted me back over to my spot under the blanket, and proceeded to eat his (slightly melted) ice cream as if nothing happened.

"Eat," he ordered. How he could see me *not* spooning the velvety lusciousness into *my mouth* when he stared straight ahead was one of the world's great mysteries.

Right. I was just supposed to eat now? As if my sides didn't still hurt. As if he didn't exponentially exacerbate my. Stinking. Crush.

Fork my life!

FIVE

I can't recall how the movie ended. I woke the next morning to the sun shining through the blinds of Lennon's window, laying in Lennon's big—and I hated to admit this—comfy bed, with Lennon's bare-chested body wrapped around mine.

I remained fully clothed and Len had one bent leg kicked from under the covers, hooked over my thighs, showing off his fully-panted self.

Okay. No sex. Good.

Yeah, my brain sucker-punched me for thinking that, too.

It had been over a year since Brian broke things off, which meant over a year since my girl parts flicked on the NO VACANCY sign. Nope. Vacant up in there. Vacant, vacant, vacant—as far as the eye could see. That last part I added for effect. I mean, unless you owned a speculum and went by the name Dr. Shivers, OBGYN, then you really couldn't see anything. But I believe I made my point.

My body wanted him.

My crush, which apparently controlled my body, wanted him.

I wanted him.

I couldn't have him, though, right? Because what did I really know about him besides he was a sexy jump instructor who sailed around the world?

Well, very sexy jump instructor.

Let's just say I gave in and had sex with him, then what? I knew going into it he was a fake boyfriend only around for a month.

My screaming crush vehemently rejected the idea of him leaving, but that was an inevitability.

How bad would it get for me if we did sex things up?

Although if I didn't, I'd still be the same fearful Kami who got made fun of behind her back by people she thought were her friends, instead of the fearless Kami who'd taken back her life. Made it whole again.

Maybe I could find real love again, not the fake kind from a fake boyfriend or the cheating kind from a real boyfriend who couldn't handle my rough patch.

I can do this... I can do this... I rolled into him, bent in, and kissed him for all of two seconds. *I can't do this...*

And I abruptly turned away, or at least I *tried* to turn away. Hard to do when the sleepy man you just tongue-assaulted grabbed on tight and wouldn't let go.

"I'm sorry. I'm sorry." I tried to apologize. I tried to protest, pushing away from him. Lennon held on tighter. And then he bent in and kissed me. No tongue-assault this time, not with me as a willing participant.

Len kissing me in the lake blew my ever-loving mind. Len kissing me in a bed in a way that distinctly felt like a prelude to sex—*with Len*—no words existed in the English language to describe this. I'd say the world, but as I didn't know all the languages of the world, that would be a pretty brazen statement on my part.

His hands began to roam blissfully up under the hem of my shirt. Caressing strokes lit my skin on fire. I used to get turned on by Brian; we had a really good sex life. But I didn't ever remember it feeling like this. In the hierarchy of turned-on-edness, *combustible* had never filled the top spot before.

"Is this going further?" he asked.

What? Did he say something? Those hands. His mouth. I never wanted him to stop. My breasts heaved with each breath. I just... I just—

"Kami, sweetheart. Is this going further? I need to know."

Oh. Um. "Yes. Much, much further." How did he expect me to think straight, let alone hear properly with the blood pounding in my ears? He gave sensation overload.

Thankfully, a thought did break through. "*Condom*," I said as a reminder. Surely someone as aesthetically pleasing as Len had a plethora of colored, ribbed and maybe even flavored ones stashed in his nightstand.

"Don't worry," he chuckled out. "I got you covered." Just as I thought, he reached over to the nightstand, opened the drawer and pulled out a handful of packets. He didn't even bother pushing the drawer closed again before he was back to giving me kisses.

And then he—*whoosh!* My T-shirt up and gone faster than a jackrabbit in a sprinting contest. As he—dear lord, lord, lord—moved his mouth down my neck, grazing his teeth lightly along the way, Len reached his hand behind my back to deftly unlatch my bra. The straps, he pulled down my arms and tossed it onto the floor alongside the tee.

When his mouth found my nip, I swore angels sang in

chorus. And when he switched to the other, trumpets joined in. This. So much this. I needed him almost more than I needed my heart to keep beating.

"Please," I whispered. "Please, I need you."

"You want me, fearless, then take me."

Take him? As in undress us? Did he want me to climb on top? To ride him like a rodeo cowgirl, where he could see all my imperfection? Could I do that?

He kissed my lips again. Deep, oh so deep, and I decided that yes. I could and would ride him. Time to channel my inner rodeo cowgirl. Get ready, I was about to make this bronco buck.

I flipped him to straddle his legs and untied his sleep pants, whisking them down his legs. The man went commando in his jammies. The man was seriously packing a zucchini in his jammies. Suddenly, I wanted a taste.

Brian liked oral, but I only ever did it when he'd asked. I didn't think I ever had the urge to just go there. Not like now. But darn, the longer I stared at it, the more I wanted to try it out. And hey, he *did* nickname me fearless.

Deep breath in... Whelp, here goes nothing. I bent my head down, wrapping one hand around the width of him, licked my lips, and I went for it. He was bigger than he looked or my mouth was smaller than I thought because we reached max capacity and I started to gag.

His eyes got huge at first contact, but then he started to gently rub my back with the hand he didn't have bent under his arm to prop his head up to see me better. "Go slow... try to center," he encouraged me.

So I centered and went slow, really taking my time to get to know him better. His beautiful eyes closed as he gripped the back of my neck and moaned these delightful little moans. "I need to move, sweetheart. Either climb on or I'm about to ravage your mouth."

That kind of sounded sexy fun, but not for our first time together. I un-suctioned my mouth, untied my pants, undressed myself, and after sheathing him in a pretty purple condom, unceremoniously climbed on top. I wasn't even sure he'd fit, but Goonies never say die, and yeah, I wasn't a Goonie, but I'd watched the movie probably a billion times (slight exaggeration) as a kid.

So after positioning him right where I wanted him, I mounted my man-stallion and almost lost my breath. Brian wasn't small by any means, but Len—*wow*—no vacancy. No vacancy at the inn. Booked up tight. I squeezed my eyes shut, adjusting to the feel of him.

And wait for it, wait for it... Yes, the unbearable feeling to move hit and I leaned back, my palms gripping his knees, and I saved a horse by riding my sky jump instructor instead.

"Yes, baby," he panted. "*Oh, f—*" He bit his bottom lip, cutting himself off.

He reached out to press my little magic fun button and my muscles seized and my head fell back, throwing me off rhythm. Len grabbed both hips in his strong hands and thrust upwards while grinding me down at the same time.

I couldn't even make a noise as the pleasure washed over me. We kept at it hard and fast. And—*oh my gosh.* Every function in my body ceased to work at once as the sound of fireworks popped in my ears and bursts of bright color, red and green and blue, flashed behind my closed eyes. I opened my mouth to scream but swore only a squeak escaped.

He flipped us, my back to the mattress, one of his knees bent, then threw my leg over his thigh and flung his other leg straight behind him, the ball of his foot digging into the mattress for traction.

It was on.

As he moved inside me I realized my life would forever be categorized, BSL and ASL, before sexing Len and after sexing Len. We climbed together up orgasm mountain and when we reached the summit, he thrust us over the edge with one final pistoning push. My battle cry could be heard across continents (exaggeration) and Martians applauded his potency. Meaning, they could hear him on Mars. I didn't know men orgasmed so loudly. I kind of thought that was a woman thing.

My legs went limp. I lost the ability to move them—not that I wanted to move. Len dropped his forehead to my chest and kissed me right between the boobage.

"Morning," he said, chuckling.

"Good morning," I answered. The muscles in my legs felt like they'd work again. He rolled off me, pulling me to wrap an arm around my shoulders. Another kiss, this time to my temple.

"Damn, baby. You're not just fearless, you're a got-damn sexual goddess." The compliment hit me in my feel spot. Not just because he called me baby and a sexual goddess, but because he censored his swears for me. Who knew he'd even paid attention enough to know I didn't just not swear, but I didn't like it when others did either? I mean, sure, he said the "D" word twice, but Rome wasn't built in a day. "I can't think of a better way to wake up."

With nothing to add to that, I let it go. "I have to work today," I said. "I'm sorry I can't do more challenges with you." And I truly meant it. I'd so rather be out and about with Len than doing just about anything else in the world.

"Call in."

"I can't. These are appointments on the books, regular clients."

"Can you clear your schedule for the next couple of days?"

"I'll try. Don't you have to jump today, anyway?" I asked.

He shrugged. "I jump when I want. Rob, the owner, is an old friend. He knows when the urge hits, I'll catch waves or take a road trip. He's always there doing paperwork, but if I call in, he takes the jumps."

It must be nice to live such a carefree life.

Why must I be so responsible? Len's body felt so warm and the deliciously naughty smell of sex hung in the air. And I knew if he gave me a half hour to recover, I'd be ready to go at it again. Which meant I had to get up. Now.

Groaning, I pushed out of his arms. Surprisingly, he got up along with me. "We showering now?" he asked.

We?

"I am," I said back.

"It's my apartment. My rules. We shower together."

Lord help me... please, please help me. I couldn't say *no* to this guy.

Instead of me leading him, he led me to the bathroom and stopped us by his shower so he could turn on the water and get the temperature just right. Oh, he got it right. Warm. Relaxing. So relaxing, I let my guard down and that was when he dropped to his knees, flung my leg over his shoulder, pushed me back against the tiles and well, to be honest, gave me the second-best orgasm of *my life*. The first being in the bed this morning.

I know I technically started it, but if he didn't stop giving these perfect orgasms, how would I possibly be able to let him go at the end of the month?

He stood, wiped off his mouth, rinsed his face in the shower spray, and then kissed me. "Thanks, baby. You taste every bit as good as I thought you would."

My whole body flushed red.

"Don't be embarrassed now," he said. "You're fearless. Besides, you have no idea how long I've wanted to do that."

And it appeared I'd graduated from *sweetheart* to *baby*. Darn him. Darn his sweet words, his zucchini, and double darn his mouth. Because they spoke those sweet words and because of the tongue to sweet-spot orgasm thing.

We cleaned up. Len gave me his tarry robe while he used old towels to dry off with.

Without any other options, I re-wore the jeans from yesterday. Len had washed and dried them for me, but since I'd slept in the undies, I had to go undie-less. Plus, usually I wore nicer slacks to work. He loaned me a purple slim-fit button-down that I tied at the waist, and I threw my hair up in a loose bun. I used the little makeup I carried in my bag and that was that.

"Ready," I said.

"Got time for breakfast?" he asked.

Jiminy Cricket, the man made jeans and a T-shirt look like a single-breasted suit.

"I could eat something quick."

He nodded and headed for the refrigerator. And while he rummaged for ingredients, I picked my phone up from where he had it charging to check my emails. My fingers crossed that my early appointment had canceled, leaving me with more quality Len time.

No luck there, but holy—the messages. Notifications from facepage and instaphoto. Every friend or acquaintance I knew, it seemed, sent messages yesterday. Liking or loving the new video and leaving encouragements like, '*You go, girl!*' and '*Kami's back*' among others.

It wasn't the skinny-dipping video, though there were some more comments on that one, too.

I clicked on it. There I was. In Coup's. Eating the hottest hot wings known to man. "Uh, Len... is there something you want to tell me?"

He looked at me, curious, over his shoulder. "I don't —*oh*... People responded to the hot wings video, right?"

"Yes. And I didn't even know there *was* a hot wings video."

"How are you supposed to show up your ex without the proof?"

Well, he had a point there.

"Besides," he said, "that was epic. I've never completed that challenge."

I smiled, contemplating that thought as the kitchen began to fill with the aroma of creamy scrambled eggs and buttered whole grain toast. Fast but delicious. Len was a cooking badarse. He even added cinnamon to his coffee grounds before he brewed it.

We ate and I legitimately wanted this, to wake up next to Len, shower with Len, and eat his delectable breakfasts for the rest of my life. This screaming crush was careening down a dangerous road.

Fake boyfriend, Kam. Fake. Not real. He doesn't want you like that.

After we ate, he drove me to the salon. "See you later, baby," he said right before smacking a big ol' kiss to my lips. One of my coworkers, Brigeeta, pounded on the window as she passed. When I turned, she had two thumbs-up for me. Len threw his head back and laughed.

Wow, that sounded sexy-wonderful.

As soon as I got inside, Brigeeta looked ready to pounce, but thankfully (and this would probably be the only day I'd ever say this) the salon owner, Dion, called a morning staff meeting so we only had minutes to set up before we opened for business.

The minute Dion's back was turned, Brigeeta launched in. "So?"

Right. Just as I opened my mouth to skirt around the answer, my first client walked in. Saved by the client.

A steady stream of regulars found their way into my chair. I was about to take a lunch when the bell over the door chimed sweetly and we all looked up. Len walked in with the most highbrow woman I could imagine on his arm. Though beautiful, she looked a good ten years older than him. If I detected Botox, then maybe fifteen.

But why would he come into the shop with a beautiful woman on his arm? That wasn't how an adoring boyfriend would act.

"Kam," he said, stopping in front of my station. "Baby, this is Meredith Lowenstein. Her husband is tech giant Brandon Lowenstein."

Okay. So my eyes might have bugged. But at least that was better than Dion drooling all over himself. Maybe he didn't actually drool, though his mouth hung open wide enough that it was possible.

"Good to meet you, Mrs. Lowenstein," I said. "How can I help you?"

"Lennon here says you are the best at what you do, and we're setting sail in less than a month. I want a new, fresh look. Something beautiful and easy to maintain, but makes me look like a million bucks when we dock at each of our destinations."

She's setting sail? Like with Lennon? As in the boat that he was captaining? "Um, I don't—"

"Please, have a seat," Dion said, cutting me off—the rapscallion. "I'm Dion. Anything you require before we start your experience?"

"Not that I can think of," she said to his back because he already had a bottle of Dom in his hand and was popping the cork.

He filled a champagne flute, handing it off to her. "Complimentary champagne." Then he walked to the back and came out with a tray of unwrapped Godiva chocolates. "Please, help yourself."

While she snacked on expensive booze and candy, I gave her the full salon treatment. From shampooing to kelp facemask to heated pore-reducing towel treatment. Finally getting to the scary part, her hair.

I pictured how I'd want *my* hair getting off a yacht in Saint-Tropez or Monaco, pictured every last detail. And hoping she and I had the same vision, I began cutting. The woman had a seriously thick volume of hair with, as it turned out, these gorgeous natural waves that changed the style slightly from my original plan but *wowee*, the end result looked amazing.

But no matter what I thought of my work, the question beckoned, would *she* like it?

"*Oh my.*" She gasped, clapping her hands to her cheeks. "You are every bit as amazing as Lennon suggested."

"Thank you." Secretly, I beamed.

"I must have you."

Uh... what?

"Have me?" I asked.

"Yes. For the trip. I cannot be expected to keep this

gorgeousness up myself. I simply must have you." Then she turned to Dion. "How much for her?"

Double what?

"I'm not for sale," I protested.

At the same Dion, ever the businessman asked, "How much are you willing to spend?" Without involving me in the conversation again, Mrs. Lowenstein opened her Versace bag and plunked down a thousand-dollar tip for me. Yes. A thousand-dollar tip. For me. Then she and Dion walked to the backroom.

SIX

I stared at the money, dumbfounded. I made amazing tips in this salon. But never a grand at one time from *one* customer.

"Breathe, baby. This is good," Len said.

Len. I blinked. "How is this good? I can't go with you." The panic rose in my voice. But before a chuckling Len with his sexy eye crinkles could answer, my traitorous boss and *Meredith* walked out from the back all smiles.

Dion spoke. "She's going to triple your annual salary for the six months you'll be gone and offered the salon a more than generous donation for the loan of my best employee. I'll water your plants."

And like Dierdre, who I considered one of my best friends, and coincidentally was a woman Dion couldn't stand to be in the same room with, Dion wasn't just my boss but my other *one of my best friends*. And he stabbed me in the back.

He couldn't loan me out.

He spent BFF nights in with me countless times over the years, where we'd give each other facials and watch rom-com chick-flicks, and talk about boys. That was mostly on him, as I had no boys to talk about other than Brian, and Brian had asked me not to talk about us to Dion—so I did it sparingly. He saw me through binge eating tubs of frozen cool whip when Brian left me. He had a key to my apartment so he could just let himself in when I was home, and to check my mail and water my plants when I went home to visit my parents.

He *could not* loan me out.

"I can't just leave for six months." I protested.

"You can and you will. We've signed a contract. Unless you wish to resign."

Blackmail. Utter blackmail. He knew I'd never make the kind of money elsewhere that I made here. Our salon had a reputation for being the best of the best.

"What about my regular clients?"

"We'll split them between the others," he said.

"Then what happens when I get back and don't have any clients?"

"Some will inevitably come back to you and I have no doubt that once they find out you're Meredith Lowenstein's personal stylist, new clients will drop at your feet."

"But..."

"No buts. Unless you're resigning today, you're off through the end of the month when you leave. Get your affairs in order because you'll be gone a long time. This is for your own good, girl."

Meredith gave air kisses first to Dion and then to me, and then she kissed Len's cheek for real before leaving the salon.

Talk about living in an alternate universe. Dion wanting me to go made sense, he liked his Italian designers too much to turn down such a payday. But how could Len think us working together for six months could end in anything but disaster? Like I needed to see him pouring his affections on other women, as if they deserved his legend-in-the-making orgasm skills. More than that, who were they to think they deserved his smile, where his eyes crinkled at the sides, or his boisterous laugh? They didn't deserve his kitchen skills. And they certainly didn't deserve the way he kissed and the way he held me, which made me feel wanted, appreciated... understood.

Even as a fake boyfriend, he'd given all that freely.

"That wasn't nice," I said.

Looking utterly confused, he grabbed my hand to tug me into his arms, holding on close and tight. "I think it's very nice," he whispered low.

I felt dizzy this close, almost drunk.

Len drunk.

"Kami, baby?" he asked.

His voice broke through the fog of my brain. "Uh, what?"

"I said get your stuff, fearless." And he kissed the hinge of my jaw. My chin. The tip of my nose. And finally my lips. He kissed in a way distinctly inappropriate for public, let alone my work.

The kissing continued right up until we heard, "*Girl...*"

We both turned to see Dion biting his bottom lip. Right. I cleared my throat in an attempt to clear my head.

"Get your stuff," Len repeated.

I jolted into action, packing up my supplies from my station and gathering my purse and favorite sweater from the back.

Dion hugged me before I left, a hug like he wouldn't be seeing me again. It moved me in a way that made me hug him back.

"Enjoy this," he said, then let me go.

I wasn't sure what he meant by that. Though he worked under the false assumption that Len actually wanted me and not that when he eventually showed his real colors with some gorgeous supermodel, I lose my marbles and end up getting fired by Meredith because she'd known Len much longer.

"Thanks," I said, instead of correcting him. What good would it do?

Len lifted the box from my hands to carry out to his truck.

"I had an idea," he said, stopping to open my door.

"Okay?"

"You up for it?"

"I guess," I found myself answering, and surprisingly, I was.

He placed my box on the floor of the backseat and drove out headed east.

Nothing existed out this way. Well, only that 'wilderness experience' park. But no, he wouldn't take me to a wilderness experience.

Except he would.

The proof of that statement slapped me in the face when he turned down the long, could-be-used-as-the-setting-for-a-horror-flick drive. The long, *long*, seemingly *never-ending* could-be-used-as-the-setting-for-a-horror-flick drive. "Your idea wasn't to take me out here to kill me so you could dispose of my body, was it?"

"How'd you guess? Now my nefarious plan is *ruined*." He made his voice high and whiny, like a pouting little girl.

The truck hit a crater, which jerked my head and sent it cracking hard against the window glass. "*Ouch*," I cried out, rubbing the side of my face where I'd hit it.

And the jerkface laughed at my pain, even as he tried to

pretend he wasn't by faking his concern. "Oh, baby..." He laughed. "You alright?"

"*No*," I shouted, then punched him in the arm, which only made him laugh harder.

Though his laughing had the added effect of making me laugh. Because whether I want to admit it or not, if the situation were flipped and Len had hit his head, I'd be doing the exact same thing.

"Let me see." He took hold of my chin to turn my face, checking it over where I'd hit it. "No bruise. Just red."

He bent in to kiss the red spot. Then he went back to driving, fiddling with the radio station to get a good song. Or what *he* thought of as a good song because in my opinion, he'd passed several.

Then the first lyrics of Bon Jovi's iconic son "Living on a Prayer" flowed through the speakers.

"*Kami likes her drinks on the rocks...With taxes and tip, she's down to one buck it's true, so true...*" Len took over for the singer.

"I don't think those are the lyrics," I corrected him. "But you be you, Len."

"What can I say? I like to make up my own."

"Well, those were interesting."

"No—*Kam, let's play truth or dare.*" Len cut himself off to sing a ridiculous chorus that did not go to the song.

And aw, heck, I couldn't stop myself. "*No Len, I'd rather wash my hair,*" I joined in.

Fist pumps and devil horns in the air, Len and I banged our heads to the beat of the music until he hit the parking lot at the end of the drive and turned into a spot, throwing the truck into park.

We opened the doors to both him and me screeching way off-key, "*I'd rather wash my hair...*"

Yeah, we weren't alone in that parking lot. Several sets of eyes turned to us. Several brows furrowed. Len cut the engine, effectively ending the disruption. Though I was guessing not before we scared off several of the woodland creatures that made their homes nearby.

He climbed out. I climbed out. We both shut our doors and I met him around the front. The glares didn't stop.

"What?" Len asked the crowd. "It's Bon Jovi," he finished, grabbing my hand to pull me faster.

I bit my lip to keep from cracking up.

Why couldn't he be a real boyfriend? My screaming crush just got screaming-*er*. Never. Never had I ever had so much fun with a guy before. Or a girl for that matter. Most people, their hang-ups kept them from enjoying life. Not Len, the man had no hang-ups.

When we reached the glass door, he nudged my side with an elbow. We put on straight faces and walked in calmly.

The inside looked every bit what one would imagine a wilderness experience lobby to look like, i.e., log cabin walls, fake trees, and stuffed animals hanging from said trees. Available for sale, of course. There was a cooler to purchase soft drinks and water. Cookbooks, which I found odd. I wasn't eating woodchuck stew or whatever they had going on between the pages. Snacks. Chips, nuts, granola. Plus artisan fudge and caramels. Then they even had consignments such as handmade soaps and patchwork fabric bags.

I could've stayed looking for a while longer, but Len had other ideas. He led me to the desk.

"Welcome," the woman behind the counter said. "Have you been here before?"

"No," Len replied.

I shook my head.

"Well, let me explain some of our features and you can decide which attractions you'd like to participate in."

"No need." Len pointed up to the board behind the woman. "We'll take two of the extreme package."

"That's pretty lofty if you've nev—"

He cut her off. "We can handle it."

"Okay, then..." She punched numbers into the cash register. "Your total comes to eighty-two seventy-three."

I kind of, sort of reached for my wallet. And he *not* kind of swatted my hand away. But that was a lot of money to spend on a fake girlfriend and I felt bad.

"Reach for that wallet again and see what you get," he warned.

I put my hands up in front of me, the universal *okay, I'll stop*. Though since I knew he'd never physically hurt me, part of me wanted to reach for my wallet again just to see what he'd do.

After stuffing his credit card back in his wallet, he dropped his arm around my waist to usher me through the revolving door that led outside. Several trails branched off from the spot where we stood. The extreme package came with four attractions. We needed to present our tickets at each attraction of our choosing, and the attendant would use a hole-punch to prove we'd participated.

Len apparently knew which attraction he wanted first because he spent all of five seconds looking at the map before grabbing hold of my hand and dragging me towards one of the trails. As tends to happen, the temperature dropped the farther in the forest we walked. Crickets and my guess, toads, chirped. Birds sang. It smelled fresh and damp. The tip of my nose went numb from the chill.

Finally, we reached a clearing and our first challenge on

this adventure. A—I used my finger to count—four-story rock wall.

"Len, I can't do that. It's too high."

"You can do it," he assured me. Well, tried to assure me.

"I can—"

"She's first." He was big on cutting people off today. Then before I could back out, he handed my ticket over to the attendant.

The attendant punched a hole in the top left corner of the thick paper, handed it back to Len and told him, "You have to wait here."

Next thing I knew I was being trussed like a Thanksgiving turkey in a harness hooked to a bungee cord, which they'd attached to the top of the rock wall. And a helmet secured to my head.

"Try to find the biggest hand and footholds. It'll take the strain off your arm muscles," the attendant said.

Then he swatted my behind to get me moving like he were a coach and I was one of his players.

Len started shouting his encouragements to me right away, though I had to ignore him to concentrate.

I stood in front of the behemoth, contemplating each move before ever grabbing the first hold. It was slow-going. I had to stop to rest every second advance. Here I always thought I was in shape, but I supposed there was a big difference between "in shape" and "rock-climbing in shape."

About halfway up, Len's encouragements sounded as if they came from beside me instead of below me. I kept plugging away. Up two, rest. Up two, rest. Up two, rest.

Until—what the heck was going on? It sounded like Len's encouragements came from *above* me now. I looked up and sure enough, a harnessed, helmeted Len waited at the top of the rock wall.

"Come on, fearless," he said. "You got this."

What could I do besides make a final great push for the top? I didn't want to disappoint Len... or myself if being honest. I took the last four advances without stopping. When I got to the top, he wrapped one arm around my waist to pull me close and planted a big, wet kiss to my forehead.

"You did it, baby," he whispered right before letting loose an ear-piercing, "*Woo!*"

I shifted in his arms, holding on to the top of the wall with one hand, just as he did, to stare out at the vastness of the forest. The trees. The sky. What a rush. In that moment, I felt like my brother was looking down on me, smiling. Tears, happy yet tears nonetheless, filled my eyes.

"This is incredible," I whispered.

"I got it all," the attendant called up to us.

When I looked down, he had Len's phone in hand.

"Did he video us?" I asked Len.

Len didn't answer, but snared me in a killer—and by killer, I mean glorious—lip lock, right before he tightened his grip around my waist and pushed off the wall. We floated down and were greeted by the attendant at the bottom, who handed off Len's phone so he could unhook us.

"That was amazing," I shouted to everyone in earshot.

"We still have three more to go." Len urged us away from the rock wall, taking us down another trail.

A ten-minute walk from the wall later had us climbing to the top of a—again I used my finger to count—this time six-story tower after getting the second hole-punch and once again being harnessed.

My thighs burned by the time we rounded the platform

to the sixth story. That had to be the most wooden steps I'd stepped in my life for a single climbing adventure. And there was only one way down from here. Len expected me to zipline down, across a large pond or small lake, until I reached ground on the other side.

I covered my eyes with both hands. "I don't think I can do this," I said, somewhat panicked.

"You're my fearless girl. Yes, you can."

But I wasn't his. I was fake his. And although fake his could probably do it, real *me* started to become dizzy. "No, Len. I don't think I can."

"Look at me, Kam."

I turned to stare deep into those gorgeous blues.

"*Kam... time to do that dare,*" he sang to me.

"*No, Len. I'd rather wash my hair,*" I tried to sing the lyrics I'd made up in the car, though they sounded weak, squeaky and flat. "Did you hear that? Flat. Which is how I'll end up if I fall. Do you really want that on your consonance? For me to *die*."

"You'd hardly be any good to me dead, fearless. But I'll concede, maybe it was the wrong song choice. Let me think." He paused for a second. "Right. I got it." Then he started singing, "*That girl she bold, she fearless don't you know...*" The next words came unintelligible because I didn't think he knew them. But then he hit the chorus, "*She a badarse mutha f—*"

I covered his mouth with my hand. He sang "arse" for me, but what did one replace the F-word with?

"Okay, okay..." I laughed. "I never heard that one."

"And you wouldn't. I made it up."

"Wow, I'm impressed."

"Good, now move your cute butt." He spun me around and shoved me off the ledge.

He *shoved me* off *the ledge.*

"*Ohmygosh,*" I screamed as I zipped down the line. The wind whipped at my face. I choked and coughed when a bug flew down my throat because I was stupid enough to scream while ziplining.

Still, nothing I'd done so far compared to the exhilaration of speeding toward the hard, packed earth while my fake boyfriend cheered behind me. There were hoots and yelps from the ground, people watching or waiting their turns.

And so caught up in the rush, I almost forgot to lift my legs at the bottom so I didn't hit them against the wooden ramp and end up with two broken legs or possibly a broken back. Last minute, I remembered and lifted, jarring to a stop when the attendant waiting to receive me grabbed my harness.

All smiles, I jumped up and down and hugged the attendant.

"That was amazing," I called to Len, who didn't have to be shoved, but *leapt* from the platform to begin his zip.

It felt like seconds slowed to millennia while I was up there, but watching him, the seconds sped up to milliseconds. Faster than fast, he touched down, much more gracefully than me. But the man jumped from airplanes for a living, so I wouldn't expect anything less.

SEVEN

THE JUMP

The man just kept upping his game. Rock walls and ziplines should have been the pinnacle, but no. Not with Lennon as my guide. From the zipline, we took the trail to the right. I smelled the heat before I felt it.

And boy, did I feel it coming off a long pit carved out in a flat area of grass and dirt. Len got our tickets punched and a pretty blonde woman led us up to said pit. A pit full of burning charcoal. Some red-hot and some whiter-hotter.

"You've got to be kidding me," I said.

"Nope," he replied.

"Uh, yeah..." I pointed to the pit. "That's not happening."

"Yes, it is."

"Take your shoes off and roll up your pant legs," this new attendant ordered.

It felt like an out-of-body experience as Len walked me over to the cement bench and held my hand while I sat. He pulled off my shoes and socks, then rolled up my pant legs. Sitting next to me, he did the same for himself. We stood and then before I could throw my impending hissy fit, he had me at the base of the pit while the blonde explained the rules.

"We suggest walking fast, but try to keep your feet flat. It disperses the heat better so you don't end up charring your skin. When you get to the other side, cool your feet off in the pool. Got it?"

I nodded. "Yes."

"Great. Remember, pressure points are bad. Now go."

And because I was apparently good at taking orders but bad at self-preservation now, I stepped onto the coals but didn't linger.

No pressure points.

Walk fast.

The heat radiated up through my feet, but oddly enough by following her directions, it didn't burn like I thought it would. More uncomfortable than outright pain. Then yeah, I did it. My feet. Hot coals. Easy-peasy. I stepped onto the grass at the opposite end of the pit, where I was ushered by a second attendant into the small in-ground wading pool to cool my toesies thoroughly.

Black coal dust drifted from my feet and dissolved from the chemicals—I smelled vinegar—in the water. The attendant let me stay standing in the pool while we watched Len walk across the pit.

He barely bent his knees and his toes were spread out wide, arms out to his side for balance, which made him look like a fast-walking Frankenstein's monster.

Did I look like that?

I doubled over laughing. So much the attendant had to move me so Len could soak his feet too.

"Never done that one before," he admitted.

My laughter died on my tongue abruptly. "*What?*"

"Yeah, that was a first." He shrugged. "And I knew they did it here, so..."

"What'd you think?"

"I'm probably not going to be a professional coal walker. But I'm glad I did it."

Hearing him say that, I admitted my truth. "Me, too."

Since there weren't any more customers yet, they let Len and me sit soaking our feet in the water a while longer. He wrapped an arm around my waist and drew me to him. I rested my head against his shoulder.

"Today was fun," I admitted.

"It ain't over, fearless. We got one more to go."

Like with all the other challenges, the attendant videoed this latest escapade for us. Messages popped up by the tens and twenties of all the people who'd seen us climb the rock wall and then zipline down on my social media accounts.

One in particular caught my eye.

Brian: *Proud of you, Kams. You look gr8.*

Hmm... I looked great, huh? Well, I wondered how New Zealand Kiki would feel about his comment. What did it matter? I had Len sitting next to me. His arm around me. My head on his shoulder. I'd never have done any of this without him. Brian could take his proud-of-you and shove it where the sun don't shine.

He never tried to help me past my issues. He'd simply replaced me well before I'd known I was being replaced.

Gah. This was bad. Mayday. Mayday. My resistance ship was going down. We'd moved past screaming crush two challenges ago. I was falling for Lennon.

I was falling for him and he was bound to break my heart. At some point someone as great as Len was bound to meet a girl he wanted for a real girlfriend. And any girl with functioning brain cells in her head would want him back.

"Ready?" he asked, placing a kiss to my temple.

"Mmm... yeah."

The final challenge I didn't understand. It started out like all the others, mainly us taking the walking trail to our destination. But our destination brought us back to the front building. Though instead of going back into the lobby, Len veered us right to a different door. Inside was a reptile house. Reptiles never scared me. Every species lived behind glass with heating lamps to keep them warm. We stopped at each of the habitats. Snakes and lizards. One handler was mid-drop with a freeze-dried mouse into a rattler's terrarium. We stayed long enough to watch it shake his namesake rattle and launch, fangs bared, at the dead rodent, swallowing it down in two gulps. The way the muscles rippled forcing the furry meal down the snake's throat fascinated me.

In the middle of the room, they'd set up a small stadium-style bench seating area. Shallow steps moved down toward a heavy-duty stone and cement table, and what looked like a coat tree for handler hooks.

Len led me down to the front, where we took the center spots. Although we were the first, it didn't take long for other people to file in and fill the seats. One main handler walked out and welcomed us. He began explaining about the hooks. The food they fed the snakes and lizards. And other interesting facts about reptiles.

Behind him, his assistants walked in one at a time, some carrying poisonous snakes in portable terrariums, and some with lizards like bearded dragons and chameleons to show off. Sitting in the air conditioning was a nice reprieve from the heat outdoors, but I still didn't understand where the challenge lied.

Then Len stood up and handed our tickets to the lead handler. He punched the last holes for us and handed them back. Len pulled me up and that was when I thought my heart would seize up.

"It wouldn't be a trip to the reptile house without getting to see the constrictors," the handler, who introduced himself as Tod, told the audience.

Three, yes, three assistants brought out six feet of reticulated python. I think Tod talked about the skin patterns. But I couldn't get myself to look anywhere but the bulge in the belly. The bulge that had begun its life as a leg connected to an incredibly large pig.

"Mollie"—what they named the snake—"loves pork," Tod announced loudly to the giggles and squeals of the audience.

Great. But I needed to know the challenge.

"To end the show, we always bring up volunteers. Today we have—" Tod paused.

"Kami and Len," Len told him.

"Kami and Len," Tod repeated louder for the rest of the audience.

Now the nerves showed their ugly, nervous faces.

"What do you do?" he asked.

"I'm a skydiving instructor," Len answered.

My turn. "I'm a stylist at an upscale salon."

"That's an interesting pairing," Tod went on. "Welcome."

I made the mistake of letting my guard down. Oh, that sneaky Tod, he called me up to stand next to him, which I did, Len taking the spot next to me.

"Put a body width between you, please?" Tod asked us.

And like fools, we did, stepping apart.

"Now Kami and Len are going to help us show you just how long reticulated pythons can get."

Excuse me?

We, *what?*

Two of the assistants picked up Mollie's tail end and draped it around Len, oh yes. *Draped it around Len.* His shoulders. But they weren't through. No, no, no... Tod and his assistant from Hades dropped Mollie's head around *my shoulders.* And Mollie felt like moving.

"If she squeezes too tightly, let me know right away," he said.

You think?

I'd have been nervous for Len, watching Mollie wrap her tail around his arm several passes if it weren't for her doing the same with her head around *my* arm. Her powerful muscles constricted, pulling Len and me closer together again. Her middle section, the one containing the pork leg, drooped between us.

My knees felt like they could buckle any minute under her immense weight, which Tod explained came out to one hundred sixty-two pounds, but as her food hadn't digested yet, she weighed in at a whopping one-sixty-five.

"I take back... every nice thing... I said about you," I struggled to say.

Lennon chuckled and the jerkface didn't look winded at all.

"If I survive this," I said, "then I'm going to *kill you.*"

"Well, now I'm torn. I want you to survive this because, you know, I've got plans for us. But I'm not ready to die yet... those same plans." And he winked at me. *The nerve.* Now he had to die on principle.

Tod kept talking, though I zoned out.

"Smile, baby," Len whispered. "You look constipated."

I shot him angry eyes.

"Make kissy lips at the camera," he continued. "Remember, this is all going up."

No, right. I didn't remember. Knowing Brian watched these, I couldn't be seen as anything less than ecstatic to be here wrapped in a giant freaky snake. Time to channel my inner video vixen.

I puckered my lips and tried for smoldering, sexy eyes aimed at the camera one of the assistants had focused on us. I didn't know if it worked, but Len certainly couldn't stop staring at me.

"...so that'll wrap up our time for today. Thank you, everyone, for coming." Tod. I forgot about Tod again.

The assistant who'd been filming us walked over to stuff the phone in Len's pocket, getting entirely too handsy in my opinion.

"Hands and feet inside the car," I warned her. Len's eyes got round right before he smiled and I felt momentarily stupid—*hello*, not really my boyfriend. But that quickly passed because at least in public, only I got the girlfriend privileges. And a hand by Lennon's zucchini definitely felt like a privilege.

"Thank you for videoing us," he said to her. "But my girlfriend is pretty possessive of me, so I'd be careful. She's unpredictable."

My mouth popped open. What did he just say—the rat ba-*ar*stard. *Whoops*. Almost broke my own code of ethics.

She froze. Stared at me. Then took a giant step back. Only two assistants and Tod lifted Mollie from around our shoulders.

Who hit on a guy right in front of his girlfriend? Not to mention now all the workers thought I was a looney-pants who'd go off at the slightest provocation. I'd have actually been pretty upset at the situation if he didn't wrap his arms around me and pull me into a hug. "Proud of you, baby," he whispered, then kissed me—slow, sweet, and every bit Len. "My fearless girl," he mumbled with his lips still pressed to mine.

"I can't believe I did that," I admitted, squeezing him tighter. *Heck yeah*, proud didn't begin to cover my feelings toward myself. And I didn't think I'd felt proud of myself in years. "What else you got?"

"Adrenaline rush?" he asked.

And well, that didn't answer my question. But when I thought about it, yeah. Absolutely an adrenaline rush.

"*Yes.*"

"Right. So we're done for the day." Releasing my hips from his hug, he reached over to hold my hand, tugging me along next to him.

I tried not to budge, putting up a fight. "What? No... why?"

He, of course, being Len, which meant being eons stronger and faster than me, scooped me up into his arms to walk us out of the reptile house. He bent his knee and pressed it against the wall to free a hand to open the door, then carried me through the lobby using his butt to push open the front glass door.

"Uh... what are you doing? Put me down."

"I will." Gravel crunched under his feet as he made his way across the lot.

"Len, put me down."

"I *will*."

Except he didn't. Not only did he *not* put me down, he had *no intension* of putting me down. People stared at us the whole way to his truck.

All I could do was wave. My face burned. "I'm not an invalid. I can walk."

"Sure you can... but I like carrying you, so quit your bi-*otching*."

Right, now I couldn't be annoyed with him. He was watching his mouth for me. That decided, I quit my biotching. We stopped at the passenger side of the truck and he stuck his hand in his pocket to produce his keys, hitting the *unlock* button on the fob. He opened the door and then put me down by sliding my bum onto the seat.

The man had thoroughly upped his demonstrative kissing game. Yesterday had been good, but it seemed today he took every opportunity to display affection. I couldn't even say PDA, because half the time we weren't in public. Now was no different. Before pulling away or shutting the door, Len bent in to brush his lips over mine. If anyone could make my heart beat erratically from a lip brush, it was Lennon. Darn. *Calm down, heart.*

Abruptly, he stole those lips from my skin that needed them and shut the door. I watched him jog around the front of the truck. He opened his door and climbed inside.

"Let's go home," he said." How about dinner and a movie?"

My eyes lit up. I could so eat. He was a mind reader. "Pizza?" I asked.

He chuckled. "Sure, we can do pizza, baby. We can have whatever you want."

EIGHT

Before driving us back to his apartment, he turned down streets I didn't recognize in a section of the city I'd never been too. An older section with a few broken-out street-lamps, boarded-up windows, uneven, cracked sidewalks, and the sour aroma of trash filled the cab of the truck.

I wrinkled my nose. "Uh, Len... I think you took a wrong turn."

"You said you wanted pizza. I'm getting pizza." He clicked on his blinker and turned one more right.

"I said I wanted *pizza*. Not *salmonella*."

"Whoa, slow down there, Ms. Judgy Judgerson. Books. Covers. Ring any bells?"

"I judge *all* my books by their covers. Cover, back blurb, first page. In that order."

He snickered as he drove one car length past an open spot, cut the wheel hard, and backed in. He pulled forward to straighten the frontend out and cut the engine. Len even made parallel parking look easy.

We parked across the street from a storefront with an

awning straight out of the 1940s. Red-and-white awning with the word *Napoli* written in green font.

"I've been coming here for years," he said. "They make the best pizza anywhere, and I've been all over the world."

"That's high praise." I slung my purse around my shoulders and opened the door because if he thought he was leaving me to sit out here, he was cracked in the head.

Len met me around the truck and took my hand. We looked both ways before crossing, though ours was the only car in sight.

A bell dinged when he pulled open the door and so much better than the trash smell outside, we were hit with the pungent, tangy aroma of onion, oregano, and parmesan. Oddly enough, no garlic.

"*Leno,*" the little old man behind the counter greeted Len. He couldn't be more than 5'1" if just and he had class one, Shar-Pei puppy-level wrinkles over his head, face, and neck. So much that the skin drooped over his eyes so I wasn't sure how he actually saw anything. Although totally bald with liver spots, he had the thickest salt-and-pepper eyebrows probably of any human alive.

"Hey, Mr. Napolitano," said Len. "How are you?"

"You bring pretty girl to see me?" The old man gestured to me with his hands but seemed to put his whole body into it.

We walked up to the counter where Len's hand moved from mine to around my waist. "Yeah, this is my girl, Kami."

"Your girl? *Mama Mia.*" The old man kissed his fingers and shot them up in the air like he was sending a kiss to heaven while speaking some super-fast unintelligible (to me) Italian. "You never bring girl. *Rita,*" he called then to someone not in the room with us. "Come. Leno brought his girl."

A thin woman with silver hair walked from the back, wiping her hands on her apron. Her olive skin tone and fine wrinkles made her appear fifty years younger than the man. "What you mean he brought *a girl*?"

She turned to look at Len, then cut her eyes to me. "So pretty. Leno, she'll give you beautiful bambinos. I can tell." And she winked at him.

Beautiful bambinos? *Awkward...*

Again the blush crept over my cheeks. I felt the burn even as I wanted to laugh. If she only knew how fake this whole thing was.

But I went along with it. After all, I'd never see these people again.

"Does this girl mean you stay instead of taking that boat out?"

"Nope. She's going with me." Len squeezed my waist and dropped a kiss to the top of my head for effect.

It worked. The effect from his little kisses and touches made *me* start to believe it was real. And I knew the truth.

Not knowing what else to do, I held my hand out. "Hi, I'm Kami."

The little old man, or Mr. Napolitano, shook my hand, gripping it firmly. "So good to meet you, *bella*."

"It's Kami, actually," I corrected him.

"No, fearless..." said Len. "'*Bella*' means 'beautiful' in Italian."

Oh. "I knew that," I lied.

When he finally let go of my hand, the woman immediately tugged me by my shirt to slam against her bosom, wrapping me in a tight, tight hug. "We don't shake hands in this family," she said.

My arms, constricted at the shoulders, stayed limp at my side. She seemed like a wonderful woman who obviously adored Len, but um... her letting me breathe would've been welcome too.

"Rita," Len said as he tried to tug me back to him. "She's turning blue."

Rita looked down with horrified expression and shoved me away. "Sorry. Sorry. I get too excited."

Turning blue was a bit of an exaggeration, but it got me the result I wanted.

"We're here for an extra-large Margherita," Len explained to Mr. Napolitano.

"Bellissimo, *bellissiomo*... Rita, you stay here, I make pie." Then in a move I did *not* expect, Mr. Napolitano moved from around the counter to pull me from Rita. "Come, bella Kami. We make pie."

Um...oh-*kay*.

And he continued to tug me back into the kitchen. I went to the sink to wash my hands, a habit still ingrained in me from my years working food service as a teenager, while the old man scrounged me up an apron.

I tied on the bleached white covering, waiting for him to finish washing up his hands. Then he took me to the table with a bowl that had a damp towel draped over it. He flipped up the towel to show off a vat of prepared dough. A scale rested to the left of the bowl, but I had a feeling the man never used it.

He pinched off a large blob and started stretching it while moving it in a circle. He had an old-school brick oven burning, set in to the back wall behind us. And it felt like a bajillion degrees radiating off that sucker.

Then he set his circle down in a pile on the flour-dusted surface in front of him and reached back into the bowl to pinch off a smaller blob of dough. "You do," he ordered me, plopping the blob down in front of me.

"Oh, I don't think..."

"No, don't think. *Do*."

Don't think, do. That was the whole point of these excursions, to do. To be the braver Kami I used to be and really, it was just pizza. What was the worst that could happen, right?

"Sure," I answered, picking up the sticky blob. "Why not?"

Mr. Napolitano showed me his technique of dusting his hands in the flour from the table along with the dough, so it wouldn't stick to my skin. And I started copying him move for move. He stretched dough. I stretched dough. Though his started to form the traditional circle of a seasoned professional while mine looked kind of like the state of Wisconsin.

"Good," Mr. Napolitano praised me, even if my work didn't warrant it. "Now throw." To show me what he meant, he tossed his beautifully round circle into the air to widen the circumference or whatever.

So I tossed mine as directed. It looked more like I tried to reshape Wisconsin's borders. I tossed it two more times, and on the third catch I heard whooping and clapping. I turned my head to see Len and Rita in the kitchen. She was doing the clapping, because Len had his phone out videoing me.

"I didn't know this was a challenge," I said.

"It's not. But I thought you might want to relive this one."

As usual, Len was right. When I turned back to the task, Mr. Napolitano had two extra large wooden peels dusted with cornmeal. The old man moved fast to pull them out and dust them in just the time I turned away. Wow.

He laid his on a peel, so I did the same with mine. Then he showed me how to sauce the pie and add the rounds of fresh mozzarella that he made there in the shop. He didn't have to tell me; I saw the pot with the steaming water and cheese curds simmering on the stovetop. I'd seen enough Food TV in my life to know that was the step before forming the balls. Finally, we topped both of ours with fresh leaves of basil.

Carefully, we walked over to the oven with our pies and slid them in. "Eight minutes," he told us.

How hot did that oven have to burn to turn out pies in eight minutes?

We folded pizza boxes while we waited. And I had to giggle at myself for getting so distracted from the delectable smell that I ruined two while the three of them talked around me. But at eight minutes, he used the peel to remove first my creation and then his, placing each directly into a box. Wisconsin never looked so good.

"Thank you so much for letting me do this," I gushed, then bent in to kiss his cheek. His eyes got huge and I realized how what I'd done could be construed. "Oh, I'm sorry. I got caught up in the moment."

That was far too familiar a gesture for only having met him a half hour ago, give or take.

"Leno, you find another girl. We keep her." And he pretend-tugged me behind him as if keeping me out of range of Len.

We all broke out the major laughs. The throw-your-head-back-and-grip-your-stomach kind.

"Nah. No other girls like Kami," Len replied. "Gonna have to fight me for her."

Instead of fighting for me, Mr. Napolitano picked up the two boxes and headed out to the front of the store. We followed in step behind him, but when we got out to the front, he simply handed the boxes off to Len.

"Can't get to my wallet," Len said.

That's when it hit me the boxes were too hot to rest on his bare arm. It would be too awkward to hold both boxes by the edges, he'd end up dropping at least one. I stepped forward to fish his wallet frim his back pocket.

The old store owner waved him away, anyway. "She worked. It's payment."

I mean, I hardly worked. I funned.

"Wow, thank you," he said.

"Thank you so much," I said too.

Rita handed me off a plastic bag with the word *Napoli* printed on the front in the same green from the awning. "You just be sure to bring her back, Leno." Then she turned to me. "Antipasto salad and breadsticks. Enjoy."

"Oh my gosh, you guys, this is too much." I began to protest even as they shoved me out the door to keep from having to hear my protests. "Thanks, again," I called back.

We walked back across the street to the truck and I waited for Len to bleep the locks to unlock it. I climbed in first and took the pizza boxes from him after I buckled my seatbelt. They were scalding hot on my lap.

I know I wore a pinched, wincing face when he climbed in because—*hello?* Hot.

"What's wrong, baby?"

"Burning... It's burning my lap."

"Shi-*ite.*" He did it again, corrected himself for me and reaching into the backseat of the cab, he rummaged around until he pulled a jumpsuit out from the floor behind his seat. "Lift," he ordered.

And I lifted the pizza boxes. He messy-folded the clothing and laid it across my lap.

I set the boxes back down. Yes. So much better.

Finally, before he started the truck, Lennon stole a kiss. A welcomed sneak attack.

"Now we can go home." He turned the ignition, shifted in to drive and fli-di-dipped out of the spot. Yes, I said fli-di-dipped. As in eased effortlessly. But I like my word better.

"They seem to really like you," I said for no other reason than to make conversation.

"Well, they really liked you, too, baby. But yeah. I was having a difficult time a few years back. I ended up there one night to get out of the pouring rain. Mr. Napolitano talked to me for hours. Made pies with me.

"He and Rita took me in, had me over for Sunday meals with the family. Robert, or as they call him, *Roberto*, is one of their twenty-seven grandkids. That's how I got into jumping. You know, his first name is actually Lorenzo. They started calling him by his middle name because he's a junior and refused to go by 'Lorenzo Jr.', 'Little Lorenzo,' or any of those they tried to saddle him with as a kid."

Talk about a small world.

And I couldn't blame him. I wouldn't want to be saddled with my father's name. Of course, I don't look much like a Jason, so...

"That's an amazing story." I desperately wanted to ask about his hard time, but if he didn't go into it, it probably meant he didn't want to share with a fake girlfriend. Some stories were meant for the real thing only. So I bit my lip on that. "Twenty-seven grandkids?" I asked instead.

"From how many kids? And I thought Rita *was* his daughter."

He chuckled through the turn, taking us back onto the main drag. "She looks good for her age, doesn't she?"

"She looks good for *any* age," I countered and reached

over to adjust the air vent so the pizza didn't cool off too much before we got back to Len's.

"She's actually only ten years younger than Mr. Napolitano. They had eight kids together."

Eight kids popped out of that tiny thing? Mind pretty much blown.

Only ten more minutes passed until we pulled into Len's parking spot in front of his condo. He climbed out and came around my side to help with the pizza while I slid down and started for the unit door.

"It's a beautiful night. Instead of going right in, you maybe want to take the pizza around back. There's a pond and a nice place to sit."

An impromptu picnic? I loved picnics. You could tell a lot about a man based on if he suggested a picnic or not. "That sounds wonderful."

"Alright... wait here. I'll go grab us some drinks."

He left the pizza box sitting on the hood of the truck and jogged up to his place. The evening felt so warm still, though not stifling. The sun started to set so the land blended in with itself, all that golden-burnt orange. No insects sang to each other yet, though the air held a low hum of electricity. Static charged. I felt it as much as I heard it. We were in for one heck of a storm probably by the middle of the night, but definitely into tomorrow. Best take advantage of the outdoors before the rain came.

The hard click of a door tore my attention from the sky. I turned my head to see Len heading for me, carrying an old blanket. I want to say it had the Star Wars logo printed on the front, but the way the folds fell over his arm, I couldn't be a hundred percent certain. Dangling from that same hand, a grocery store bag. The outline of cans pushed against the thin plastic, letting me know that was where he kept the drinks he'd gone in for.

I carried the bag with the breadsticks and antipasto salad. He picked up the pizza boxes, balancing them on the blanket with the edge of cardboard pushed right up against his chest.

"This way," he said as he began walking toward the side of the building. His had upstairs and downstairs units. Each unit had direct outside access, like walking up to a house. No hallways like in my apartment building.

We rounded the brick-and-vinyl-sided exterior and maybe fifty feet away, the pond spread out for our enjoyment. None of the other residents had yet decided to take advantage of the night and the view. And what a view. With little to no breeze, the surface of the pond appeared as smooth as a sheet of glass.

The closer we walked, the stronger the scent of pond water and humidity hit us, combining pleasantly with that of the pizza in Len's arms. My mouth watered.

We found a perfect spot under a late-blooming magnolia tree. Another layer of beauty and fragrance to set the scene. It rested in that perfect zone—close enough, but not too close, to the lake for us to enjoy all that surrounded us.

"You want to hold the boxes a sec?" he asked, handing them over before I answered. So rhetorical.

Careful to grip them by the edges, so as not to burn my hands, I held on while Len set the drink bag on the ground, unfolded the blanket—Star Wars, just as I'd thought—and spread it over the supple grass. Before he sat, he took the pizza back and waited for me to sit.

Once situated, he pulled a couple cans of a sparkling "hard

water" beverage for each of us out from the first bag. Then he pulled the antipasto salad, breadsticks—and Rita had even packed two thick paper plates and plastic forks for us, which he pulled out from the second bag, handing one set off to me.

Carb city—*no*, carb universe. We transported to a delectable carb-filled universe and I loved every second of my visit. It was no secret I liked to keep the veg-to-carb ratio of my meals higher with the veg. But we'd had such a wonderful day, and I felt like I could eat my own foot with my hunger reaching DEFCON two after exerting so much energy today. Plus, I felt no urge to hide my bread-loving persona under some false pretense of trying to impress him. If he didn't like it, he could stuff it. I mean, he was "dumping" me at the end of the month. So what did it matter?

I plucked two buttery, oregano-and parmesan-crusted breadsticks from the smaller box, then used my fork to pile antipasto salad onto my plate. Lastly, I went for the Margherita. The cheese oozed and dripped, along with oil and sauce, and I never wanted to leave this carb universe.

Before doing anything else, I bit off a large chunk of the triangle point and honest-to-goodness moaned.

The slices had cooled off enough on the drive so as to not scald my mouth. After chewing sufficiently and swallowing, I looked up from my plate to thank Len and noticed him not eating. He sat with an empty plate watching me devour my food.

A sudden bout of self-consciousness hit. "Not hungry?" I asked, setting my plate down on my lap.

Not answering right away, he leaned forward and used his finger to swipe across my cheek, next to my mouth. "Got some sauce on you," he said, then stuck the finger in his mouth and sucked it clean.

I reached back into the bag Rita sent with us to pluck a small pile of napkins out, using one to wipe my face.

"Are you going to eat now?" I asked uncomfortably.

"Oh, I could definitely eat," he answered. But I got the distinct feeling he wasn't talking about pizza or salad.

NINE

I swallowed. Hard. What else could I do? Len's gorgeous stare enraptured the strongest of women on the best of days. So when he caught you with that next-level *look*, all heated and lustful—no can defend.

And what he pinned me with right now definitely constituted *the look* if ever I saw it.

"Your, *um*, food's going to get cold." As lame as it sounded, that was the best I could come up with. Hey, I challenge anybody to speak beautiful, thought-provoking prose in the face of Len's *look*.

"Put your plate down, Kam."

Uh... what?

When I didn't react, he repeated himself. "Put the plate down, Kam."

No. I could not put the plate down. The plate remained my only barrier between Len and deliciously bad decisions.

He rose to his knees, his empty plate spilling onto the blanket, and crawled over to me, placing my full plate on top of the pizza box. Then with his arms wrapped around me, he lowered my back to the blanket, his lips hitting mine at the same time my back hit the ground.

Those angels singing in chorus and trumpets sounding from this morning were joined by Satan's low country, Cajun jazz band out here in the wide open. Even if he—Len, not Satan—hadn't started removing any pieces of clothing yet.

I swore my possessed legs opened to allow his hips to fall between them completely of their own accord. Or Satan's. I was not the get-it-on-in-public type of girl.

Len pulled his lips away. "No one can see you from here, not with the dark descending. The tree, shadows, and the way the light hits the back building, we're covered." He bent in to kiss me again. "But I won't ask you to go further than you're comfortable with."

With my rational mind visiting the Grand Canyon or maybe the Baja Peninsula of Mexico, I found right then, being in Len's arms, that I was comfortable with a whole lot I wouldn't normally have been.

It's safe to say things got a little heated, and Len was more than happy to remove some of my clothing to help cool me off. Though, through the magic of his lips, the opposite occurred and I got even hotter. *He* actually stopped us before it went too, too far. And once I regained my senses, I was actually pretty glad of it.

As he'd removed a bit more clothing from me than I had him, while I put myself back together, he loaded up his plate with Napoli's wonderful dinner. Then, sitting by the pond on a beautiful summer night, I ate the best cold pizza, no-longer-soft breadsticks, and soggy salad of my life.

When the breeze started blowing in, chilling my arms faster than I was able to rub the cool away, we packed up our trash and rolled up the blanket. Then, with my head resting on his shoulder, Len and I strolled back to his condo.

He let us inside, dumping the boxes in the trashcan by the back door. "Why don't you get ready for bed while I close things down? Just wear the T-shirt you wore last night."

It was only a few minutes later that he walked into the bedroom, pulled a clean pair of sleep pants from a dresser drawer, dropped trou to pull them on, and belly-flopped onto the bed, causing us both to bounce. Then he got silly, handsy-touchy as he situated himself under the covers next to me.

"Has anyone ever told you that you're so much better than a body pillow?" he asked as he draped a leg over my leg and an arm over my arm, essentially trapping me underneath him. And I had to admit, even if only to myself, that *he* was the better pillow.

He pecked my cheek, then whispered, "Night, baby."

I might have possibly sighed and closed my eyes to try and sleep. Ah, Lennon... jumper out of airplanes, maker-upper of lyrics to Bon Jovi music crooner, and best fake boyfriend possibly ever.

The next morning my eyes blinked open to see Len staring at me, big, cheesy smile smiling down on me.

"What's with the grin?" I asked instead of granting him a *good morning*.

"Nothing... well, no, it's something. I think we should take the day off. Go out, have some fun."

"Haven't we been having fun?"

"Yes, but our fun had a purpose. And everyone knows too much fun with a purpose quickly turns to fun-work. We're shooting for fun-fun today."

I pushed up to sitting. "Everyone knows, eh?"

"Everyone," he agreed.

But we had a problem. I lacked the proper leaving the house attire. As in, I'd been wearing the same pants for a few days now. "I need clean clothes. Those jeans could get up and walk on their own. No legs required."

"Well, it's a good thing I asked your boss, Dion, to stop by your place and pack a bag, while you were in the back finding the box to pack your stuff in. The idea hit when he said he'd water your plants. I figured he had a spare key."

Um... "*What?*"

"He seemed super excited about doing me this solid. I like him, you know. You need friends like him in your life. I got his number, then texted him my address."

"Again, *what?*"

"Check the closet. Some days I'm brilliant. Apparently, yesterday was one of those days."

Pushed up from the mattress, I stormed over to the wall closest to the foot of the bed (even though not mad, more confused) and threw open the closet door half-expecting my *a-ha!* moment proving he had not spoken with my boss, to which he'd respond with a "*Ha ha! Fooled you.*"

But I didn't get an *a-ha* moment. My pretty hot pink, lemon yellow, and apple green paisley print travel bag sat on top of a pile of shoes on the floor.

"He dropped it on my front stoop while we were out back picnicking last night. I left it out by the sofa and brought it in here last night when I got up to pee."

"Why didn't you just take me back to my place? Why go through the bother?"

"Frankly speaking, I was afraid if you went home, you'd decide to stay there, and I like you here with me."

He liked me here with him? I didn't know what to do with all that sweetness. And he was right, despite how much fun we'd been having over the past couple of days, I'd have probably found a reason to stay home. Like to freak out over the fact that I was to set sail with Len at the end of the month as Meredith Lowenstein's personal stylist. I blinked my eyes several times hoping to blink away the tears. It didn't work. So I took the only option left to me, grabbed the handle of my travel bag, and hauled butt to the bathroom.

Dion had hooked me up the way only a BFF could. He knew everything about me—my favorite outfits and how I did my hair. Twenty-five minutes later, I emerged from the shower scrubbed, hair thrown back in a ponytail, fresh makeup applied, clean clothing on my body and well in control of my emotions.

Len must have showered in the other bathroom as he sat on the sofa, one leg crossed over his knee, sporting some killer dark jeans, a light blue button-down with tiny white horses embroidered over the whole shirt, his sleeves turned up and these upscale slip-on tennies. He dressed like a young urban professional. The kind of guy who frequented cider microbreweries instead of beer, had a wine of the month club membership, and snacked on avocado toast points.

The look worked on him in a big way.

"Hey, fearless. You look beautiful today, baby." He stood and walked over to wrap an arm around my waist and pull me in for a cheek kiss.

I was no slouch. Today I decided to go full-on girly. I wore a pretty white sundress with overly large pink roses printed on the fabric, the most comfortable pair of nude-colored wedge sandals in the known universe, and a white three-quarter sleeve fitted denim jacket thrown over top in case I got chilly. Yes, we were in the middle of summer, but as Len had yet to reveal our destination, how could I know if the place he'd choose for us to go jacked up the air conditioning?

"Thank you," I responded. I *felt* pretty today. Felt happy today. So it was safe to say that Len picked a good day for our fun-fun adventure.

"Shall we?" he asked as he moved us to the door.

We landed first at a pancake house. So many varieties of delectable pancakes and like twenty syrup flavors. He and I had so much in common. I mean, he drove us there without asking for input. As if it were a given that I'd love the place because he loved the place. He'd been right. Pancakes are life. After that stop, we moved next to a little mom-and-pop coffeehouse, where he got me a salted caramel mocha. Yes, those exist and mine was phenomenal.

Over an hour on the highway later, he clicked his blinker and took an exit that led to a zoo. I hadn't been to a zoo in years.

Len paid for us both again, even though I tried to pay for my own ticket. Then we spent the next couple of hours having a blast. In front of the monkeys we took a selfie of us together, puffed-out monkey faces, posed in our best monkey-impersonating poses.

Another visitor took pictures of us pretending to run screaming away from the lions. Len had quite the sense of humor, which caused me to crush even harder. How could I not?

When I got too warm wearing my jacket, Len carried it around the park for me. About halfway through the day, we stopped to get a snack. He paid about four dollars each for two bottles of water and bought us a large box of what they called zoo-corn, which was caramel corn with candy-coated chocolate-esque carob rounds, nuts, dried blueberries, and coconut flakes.

I didn't remember ever having so much fun at the zoo.

We left about five o'clock and drove over an hour home. By the time we made it back, after all the fresh air, sun and walking around, my stomach was on the verge of consuming itself.

The need to tell him so evaporated when he turned toward the section of downtown where all the fancy-schmancy restaurants, eateries, and bistros clustered for our dining convenience.

He parked in one of the downtown's many paid parking lots and we walked the block and a half to the place he wanted us to eat.

A place called Ceibo.

I'd never been here before, but even without the sign telling us so, I knew it served nouveau Argentinian cuisine. Seeing as I'd never tried *old*-veau Argentinian cuisine, I got pretty excited.

He held the door open and I stepped inside. His hand found the small of my back as we moved into line. There were two couples ahead of us, the front-most couple being led away by a server. The next couple moved up in line, up to the hostess counter. We moved up a spot, too.

"Don't you need a reservation for this place?" I asked.

"Yep," he replied, wearing a Cheshire cat grin.

"I'd love to go here, but I'm super hungry. We'll be waiting—"

The jerk pressed a finger to my lips to shut me up and moved us up another spot so we stood in front of the hostess counter.

"McCartney, party of two."

McCartney? That was interesting. Here I'd spent two nights with the guy and never thought to learn his last name. Gone on countless adventures with the guy and *never thought to learn his last name.* Moreover, what did that say about me? Was I confusing fearless with reckless, *again?*

Len pressed his hand to my back to get my attention. I looked up to see him and his concern visible through his downturned mouth and the crinkles at the sides of his eyes.

"You okay?" he whispered. "You look far away."

"Just thinking about some stuff."

"Not tonight, fearless. Tonight, is for fun, which means you put all that other stuff out of your head."

I supposed I could do that, though, something continued to niggle at the back of my mind. I'd have to think more on it later.

The hostess ran a finger down the built-in tablet screen and pressed on his reservation. A moment later, a server, this one a woman, greeted us.

"Hello. Welcome to Ceibo. I'm Lydia and I'll be your server tonight."

We followed Lydia to a table tucked in the back corner. The room was dark with real and painted-on-the-wall palm trees. The painted palms surrounded a twilight beach scene and they played the sound of water lapping the shore. Deep blue lights strung around the room twinkled and gave the appearance of the nighttime sky.

Ambiance. The man knew how to pick a restaurant.

If this was how he treated a fake girlfriend, imagine how he treated the real ones.

We ordered cocktails first off. Mine, a Campari, citrus, peachy dream in a glass that went down way too fast and easy. Our server brought a second out for me before our appetizer came out. It was grilled cheese—like not the sandwich but an actual slab of cheese that had been grilled. They had us spread it on crusty chimichurri bread.

Len and I gorged ourselves on Argentinian flavors. And for dessert we ordered this—*goodness*—almost a tiramisu but made with dulce de leche, Argentinian chocolate and yerba mate.

No words existed for how good the meal tasted, and the conversation between Len and me flowed freely. Mostly a recap of our fun at the zoo and stories from some of his travels. We kept it light. Fun. And then it happened. I was maybe three bites from finishing my dessert when I heard it.

"*Kami?*"

I ignored her.

She persisted. "Kami, *oh god*, I thought that was you." Dierdre, the traitor, walked up to our table uninvited and acted like I hadn't called her out—well, Len posing as me hadn't called her out in that text.

There was a man I didn't recognize with her, not Rex, the last guy she'd been dating before I cut her out of my life.

"And who is this?" she asked, ogling and appraising Len.

He held his hand out for her to shake. I glowered. Her stupid hand might contaminate him with her backstabbing betrayal.

"I'm Lennon."

I squeezed my hands into tight balls on my lap as she leaned in a bit too close, oblivious to her date standing there, flashing her cleavage.

"Lennon," she said. "I like it. I'm Deirdre. Kami and I have been friends for years."

Len looked at me and then back at Deirdre. My heartbeat sped up even as I sat waiting to see what he was going to with that information.

"Deirdre?" he asked. "*The* Deirdre?"

She smiled cockily, as if him knowing about her made

her special somehow, that is until he metaphorically went right for her throat with teeth bared.

"The Deirdre who made friends with her cheating ex's new bi-*otch* behind her back and never bothered to tell her the man was a cheating bastard?" Then he looked to me. "Sorry. I don't have a replacement for bastard."

Her mouth dropped open. I covered mine.

Len wasn't done. "You call that friendship? That was a biotch move that had nothing to do with friendship. It takes a pretty low-class person to pull that on a friend."

He just called Deirdre a biotch and low-class. I looked to her date to see if this night was going to end in fisticuffs. The date stood to the side laughing.

Deirdre wasn't.

"I see the priss has you censoring—"

"*She* doesn't have me do anything." He cut her off. "I do it because she doesn't like it, and I care about her. *That*, you see, is what friendship is."

Why couldn't he be real? Because that—that was so believable. It meant a lot for him to stick up for me and— what the heck—I stood up and walked around the table, bumping Deirdre out of the way, to bend down and kiss him. Nothing pornish, but enough to relay my thankfulness.

"Everyone will hear about this," she threatened behind us, but who even cared? I kind of hoped she did spread the word. Especially since I'd be gone for six months soon, which meant I wouldn't have to deal with the fallout from when Len broke up with me. I could post fewer and fewer pictures of us together until our *relationship* faded into obscurity.

Thanks to Dierdre, I had the perfect out.

As I was so happy about this revelation, I continued to kiss Len. When we broke apart, Deirdre and her date had left and Lydia, our server, waited off to the side with our check. In an instant, once I realized we'd been making out in public, my skin heated with embarrassment.

"I uh... can't believe I did that," I said in sort of a mutter. Yes, the mutter of a shocked woman.

"Baby, that was phenomenal. You have my permission to do that *anytime* you want." And he wrapped one arm around me while taking the check. "Thanks," he said to the server.

Never letting me go, which meant pulling my butt onto his lap, Len reached into his back pocket for his wallet. He set it on the table, flipped it open, and slid a card out. Sliding the card into the leather check holder, he handed it back to Lydia, who turned to cash us out.

A text pinged my phone while we waited for Len's card to be returned. I fished the phone from my purse to check it.

Brian. Oh, for crying out loud, when Deirdre said she'd tell everybody, I figured she'd at least wait until after appetizers.

I could not deal with him tonight.

TEN

I ambled out of the bedroom, drawn by the rich aroma of dark roast Columbian brew. Something I bet most people wouldn't guess about Len was that he made coffee like nobody's business. In a real relationship, he'd be elected official coffee brewer.

"Hey, baby. Come have a seat." He handed me off an overly large mug of the magic brown liquid as I passed him on my way to the bar. During the handoff, he pressed a sweet kiss to my temple.

How did he manage to be so sweet and perfect and able to keep up the pretense even when we weren't in public?

Breakfast fare for this morning turned out to be lox and bagels, with the spread on individual plates laid across the bar top. The toaster popped and he pulled two piping-hot bagel halves, buttered them, set them on a plate for me, and slid it over.

Cream cheese, lox, onion, tomato, and capers for each of us later, he sat next to me and I could tell he had something on his mind. It was weird. Len, in the time I'd known him—

especially in the time I'd *really* gotten to know him—never held back. I didn't think he could hold back if he tried.

"What?" I mumbled around a mouthful, and I picked up a couple of the capers that had rolled off, sticking them in the soft, pulpy part of the tomato to keep them in place.

"We're leaving in a month," he said.

"*Yes.*" I drew out the word. "I'm quite aware of that."

"Then we'll be gone for six months."

"Again, not new information."

"I think we should pack you up today and move you in here."

My mouth dropped open. I set my bagel I'd picked up for another bite back down on the plate. Ran my tongue along my teeth to make sure I wouldn't spit food out when I yelled at him, and then I yelled at him. "*What the heck?*"

It might have been a slight overreaction, but I contest *what the heck?*

"Move in with you?"

"Now." He patted the air. "Hear me out. Why should you pay six months of rent and utilities when you won't be home? That's wasting money. Plus, isn't that where you were living when you and the ex were together?"

I shook my head *yes.*

"I thought you were trying for a fresh start."

"I am."

He shot me this *well?* look. As if what he proposed was the obvious next step in my *get Kami back* life plan.

"You'll be paying rent here for the six months we're gone." Yes. That was a good argument.

"I own this place. Outright." His face darkened. "Bought it with the money I got when... never mind. Anyway, I only pay taxes, utilities, and association fees. Heck of a lot less than you pay in rent."

"Where will I live when we get back?"

"Kam, baby, we'll find you a better place. But if we're going to get you moved out, you have to get your notice put in today so they don't charge you another month's rent."

"I don't know the policy. I'd have to check on how much notice I'm supposed to give."

"Okay." He ran his hands through his hair. "Even if they charge you another month, it's smarter to move you out now rather than at the end of the month when we're trying to get all the last-minutes done."

Right, so he had a point. A good one actually...

"And you really don't mind? Me staying *here* with *you* for the rest of *the month*? Because once I give up my apartment, if you get sick of me, you can't kick me out."

"I won't get sick of you."

"You might get—"

"Kami, I won't get sick of you. Now say you'll move in here so we can get ready and get your stuff."

Getting rid of my apartment was kind of a big decision to make on the fly, but hadn't I been trying to get back to the old me? Get back the girl who jumped in head first because you only live once?

Fear was the only thing stopping me. And all that fear brought to this party was a cheating ex and a backstabbing friend.

If I said yes, what would the pros be? Len's company. We had a lot of fun together. His breakfasts. The man knew his way around the kitchen. His big, comfy bed. I tended to like to snuggle at night and these past few Len had been better than a body pillow. The sex. Okay. There, I said it. The sex. Len is, was, and probably forever shall be extraordinary in the booty department and he seemed to enjoy what I gave in return.

I'd gone so long without it that I just didn't feel ready to go back to a sexless life.

Down with a sexless life, I shouted in my head. Then to my utter mortification, *"Down with a sexless life,"* I shouted out loud.

He threw his head back and laughed. "I wholeheartedly agree. Sexless life, bad. But what does that mean?"

"It means that I'm putting in my notice."

"So I assume you plan to take advantage of me while you stay here? Because I'm totally down with that."

Embracing my boldness, because it was just that easy with him, I smiled. "Yes. Yes I am."

"We should kiss on it to seal the deal."

Kiss on it to seal the deal? We went at it like a couple of teenagers on a curfew time crunch. Then we cleaned up breakfast and he led me back to the shower, where it took us a bit longer than intended to get ready for the day.

But eventually we made it out of the house.

He dropped me off out front of the complex office. And left me to go give my notice while he left to buy boxes.

I walked from the office over to my apartment and let myself in. I got hit with the weirdest sensation. Like, the space was familiar but didn't really feel like my home any longer. No more Crazy Kami. Introducing onto-bigger-and-better-things Kami. Okay, that was kind of a mouthful. I needed to come up with a better new nickname to use when telling my former friends to suck it.

My phone pinged stating that I had a new email. Freaking Brian *again*. No contact for over a year and now, when he thought I landed myself a new man, he decided to talk to me? No. Absolutely no. I swiped to the left on the message and hit delete. He could stuff his *'good for you,*

Kam' and '*I'm proud of you, Kam'* right up his handsome-though-not-nearly-as-handsome-as-Len's nose.

By the time Len made it back to my apartment, I'd cleaned out my entire closet. Dresser drawers. Bathroom medicine cabinet. And I'd stripped the bed and tossed the bedding into baskets to be washed.

He went to work on my kitchen while I packed all that stuff into the boxes he'd folded for me. As I had less stuff in my bedroom to pack than he did in the kitchen, I made my way out there to help.

We worked for hours. At about half-past four, Dion and Brigeeta showed up with bottles of Prosecco and pureed peaches for bellinis along with platters of frou-frou finger foods such as stuffed mushroom caps and blini with crème fresh and caviar. Len had called Dion when he'd gone to get the boxes. Dion called Brigeeta. They came right after work.

Dion's newest fling owned a catering company and could pretty much be considered a culinary Einstein. I ate my body weight in delicious hors d'oeuvres and we all got snockered to the point that we laughed and fell on each other more than we packed my belongings.

I was so going to miss working with these two for half-a-freaking-year.

Brigeeta found my board game collection on the top shelf in my hall closet and pulled them down. We moved from drunken Pictionary to drunken Twister (or *Twishter*, as Dion pronounced it now that he'd made it to the slurring-his-words portion of the evening).

Later that night Henri, the newest fling, showed up with leftovers from an event he'd catered earlier in the day. Creamed chicken and herbed potatoes. Haricot Verts, which is really a fancy name for French green beans, yeast rolls and triple chocolate cake.

This was what friendship was about. How could I have been so foolish about Dierdre? How could I have mistaken what she and I had for what I continued to have with these amazing people in my apartment tonight? When I got things wrong, I really got them wrong.

Eventually, we'd all drunk way too much for any of us to drive home, so I unpacked blankets. Dion and Henri took the pullout sofa. I had an inflatable air mattress for Brigeeta and Len and I took the bedroom.

We passed out pretty much on contact with the pillows. Again, I rolled into Len. I know because when I woke the next morning we were holding each other. And hungover. Or, at least, I was. This was the first time since we'd started spending the nights together that I'd woken up before him and he hadn't pretended to be sleeping just to see what I'd do next.

Carefully, I extracted myself from his arms and the bed, making my way into the living room. I expected to see my friends passed out like Len. Instead, they'd woken and decided to avoid any morning-after-party interactions and had already slipped out. Brigeeta's air mattress was deflated, her blankets folded on top. Dion and Henri's sofa bed transformed back into a regular old sofa.

We were back to just me and Len.

"Mmm... morning, baby." Speak of the devil, Len appeared in the hallway at the mouth of the living room.

"Good morning."

As I looked at him, I felt grateful to the universe for bringing him to me. Beautiful even more on the inside than the out, and the out was pretty darn beautiful, Len made me feel special. I really hoped we could remain friends at the end of this lunatic experiment.

"Let's go home, Kam. You have enough stuff there for now. I think after spending the day packing, we should have some more fun. What do you say?"

"What are we going to do with all this stuff?"

He shrugged. "We'll integrate what you want around and store whatever stuff of yours or mine that we aren't using right now. Each condo comes with an extra-large storage unit. We'll make it fit."

"Well, okay then."

"Come here and kiss me first," he said.

I obliged.

When we ended the lip-lock, he swatted my butt. "Get your shoes on. We'll come back tomorrow with a truck to move this stuff out."

After popping a couple of ibuprofens from my purse, the ones from my apartment already having been packed, I slid on my shoes and waited by the door for Len to do a sweep-through to determine how many more boxes we'd need.

Then we headed home, where he let me shower first.

As directed, I pulled on a pair of shorts and a cute scoop-neck T-shirt, and brought socks along with me. I didn't quite know what to make of this because I had on my sandals. That was the directed part, to not wear a skirt or dress and bring socks. This meant Len had a definite idea of what he wanted us to do today.

He dressed similarly. Even down to the socks.

The last thing before leaving the condo, Len packed us snacks and water bottles.

We stopped off for coffee and pastries because we both

needed them and he knew me sufficiently well by this point. Then, oddly enough, he turned into the parking lot for Stride Sporting Goods. Why would he stop there?

Well, I thought I'd wait in the car. Guess who was wrong?

"C'mon, Kam. You have to come in for this." He slid out, shut his door, and jogged around to open mine for me.

Together we walked into the sports store and he directed us to the back, where they held a large selection of shoes.

My eye caught on a cute pair of pink runners, though I didn't have much time to look because he dragged me to a completely different section. One with boots. Hiking boots, to be exact. I'd never been a hiker, per se, but I knew hiking boots when I saw them.

"Sit," he ordered, but sort of pushed me down onto the hard bench thing they had in the center of the aisle so I didn't have a choice. "Shoe size?" he asked.

"Seven and a half," I answered.

He plucked an expensive-looking pair of boots from the shelf and bent down to my feet like a shoe salesman.

"Need the socks, baby."

Those I'd stuffed in my purse. So I opened it and pulled the thick cotton out, handing it over to him. Len proceeded to unlatch my sandals and pull the socks on me, then he stuffed each foot into the boots.

"Walk around, see what you think." He stood when I did, hands to his hips, and watched me walk around the shoe aisle breaking in the boots.

"Perfect," I said.

"Good. Wear them out."

I put my sandals in the boot box and after waiting for

Len to find a pair, try them on and decide to buy, we checked out and headed back to the truck.

An hour later, he turned into a gravel parking lot out in the middle of nowhere.

"I'm not skinny-dipping again," I said, something he had to be well aware of. The last time hadn't ended too well for us. Though I wouldn't be on this adventure with Len if not for taking *that* plunge (pun intended), so I didn't hold too much animosity in my heart over the fiasco.

He laughed. "No. We're not skinny-dipping. Just going on a hike."

Now it was my turn to laugh. "A hike? That seems a bit tame for you."

Slinging the backpack over his shoulders, he exited the cab, so I did too. Len met me at the front of the truck and took my hand, leading me up to where a dirt trail started.

"This is just practice. It's a beautiful day and we were cooped up all day yesterday packing."

"Wait—practice for what?" I stopped walking, tugging on his hand to stop him.

"Oh, did I forget to tell you? We're going camping."

"Camping? No... *no*." I vigorously shook my head. "I don't camp."

Len swatted my butt to get me moving again, so I swatted his back.

He chuckled. "You didn't climb rock walls, hold pythons, or walk hot coals before either."

Well, shoot. He had a really good point.

"Okay, I guess we're going camping. But please tell me there's at least a tent."

"Yes, baby, I have a tent."

We spent the rest of the day hiking the trails and getting lost when we wanted to. Every so often, Len or I would snap a picture, not really for anyone else's benefit like the videos, for our own enjoyment to look back on.

Both of us were so tired and sweaty after our time outdoors that we ordered sub sandwiches, chips, and pickles from a local sub shop and crashed, watching movies until we fell asleep.

This time Len made sure to pull out a comedy, so no tears. Well, I'll amend. There *were* tears, but only the laughing kind.

We got up extra early the next morning and drove to the truck rental place. One of us probably should've looked up the hours of business first because we spent twenty-five minutes waiting for the place to open just so we could rent a stupid truck. Then, just the two of us, we spent the whole day loading up boxes at my apartment and unloading them either into Len's condo or his storage unit. Some things we donated to a second-hand store.

He'd decided we were taking off to camp for the week, come first light.

I insisted we needed time to plan and prepare.

"If we forget it, then we don't need it," he argued.

In the battle between Kami and Len, Kami lost.

Come first light, true to his word, the alarm clock buzzed too loud to be allowed to survive, and I chucked a pillow at it.

My body was sore from all the physical activity yesterday.

"Come on, lazy bones. Shower, dress. We got us a camping trip to go on."

I showered, brushed my teeth, dressed in a pair of pink cotton shorts, white tank, and my sandals—making sure to pack my new boots and plenty of socks.

Forty-five minutes later, we were on the road because

he promised me a greasy, so-bad-for-you fast food breakfast if I hurried.

And the place we were headed to offered cheesy hash brown bites. One moved with lightning quickness for cheesy hash brown bites.

That's all I'm saying.

ELEVEN

"We're going where?" I was not nearly greasy-food drunk enough to learn that we'd be spending the next eight hours in a truck driving up to the Upper Peninsula, or what we Michiganders have affectionately nicknamed the UP.

"Relax, Kam. You'll love it."

"I'd love a three-hour drive better." I protested by folding my arms across my boobs and raising an eyebrow, trying for intimidating.

But I guessed my intimidating needed more practice because he chuckled, reached over to wrap his hand around the back of my neck, and pulled me closer to him so he could kiss me.

Mmm-hmm. *Kiss me.*

This fake relationship would never work if he didn't take my objections into consideration.

Though I loved the way he kissed. And I supposed it wouldn't be so bad to spend the day driving up north with Len.

So yes, I relented. Is that not the worst? I wussed out... because of *a kiss.*

Several hours into the trip, we stopped at a souvenir shop with a wooden pirate ship out front for kids to climb on. I didn't think pirates were really a thing on the Great Lakes, but since we'd seen signs for the past ten miles telling us to make sure and stop here, we took the exit.

Len, the big kid, climbed on the pirate ship, hanging off the mast. I laughed so hard, I thought I'd pee myself as he posed for me. My hands shook and the first several pics came out blurry. The two kids waiting to climb aboard and their mother weren't too happy with us.

Eventually, I had to drag him off.

"Come on, big boy," I cajoled. "I'll buy you a souvenir inside."

His eyes, I kid not, lit up.

He wanted a Mackinaw sweatshirt, but we weren't in Mackinaw City yet. You can't buy a sweatshirt of a place you aren't in. It's an unwritten rule. One doesn't buy a Chicago shirt when in Winnetka. As the man was a seasoned, *seasoned* traveler, he should have known this. So we settled on a pirate hat and a promise that we'd stop in the city so he could get his sweatshirt.

The breeze picked up the farther north we traveled. Hot temps but chilled breeze. Welcome to paradoxical Michigan. That should be our new slogan.

I had to admit, you couldn't beat the area for pretty. Trees, a whole lot of birch that I could see from the highway, with leaves in full forest-green grandeur.

About five miles out from the straits, the top of the Mackinaw Bridge appeared. I hadn't been here in years and the idea of being here again got me a bit giddy. The closer we drove, the bigger the bridge appeared. I turned off the air conditioning and rolled down the windows so we could smell the lake air of mostly Lake Huron, but as Huron and Michigan joined under the bridge, it was both.

Len took the exit leading us into the downtown area of the city. Mackinaw, for those who've never been, is about as touristy as a city comes. But so worth it with the views of the bridge, the lakefront, the lighthouse and fort, and the port docks to take the ferry over to the island. Oh yeah, Michigan islands, especially Mackinac Island, could be considered some of the prettiest in the country.

I made a mental note to beg for us to spend at least one day on the island on our drive back. But right now, we had a mission. Well, we had four. Len just didn't know about three of them. One: Find a sweatshirt place. Two: Eat pancakes. I mean, he could eat anything he wanted, but I desired pancakes piled with fruit, dripping with syrup, and sprayed with whipped cream. My mouth watered and my stomach grumbled thinking about that. And if I remembered correctly, Mackinaw had some delicious pancake houses. Three: Find good coffee for the next leg of our drive. Four: *FUDGE*. Nobody, and I mean nobody, visited Mackinaw without partaking in their so-famous-it-was-made-into-an-ice-cream fudge.

We parked in the center of the downtown and walked up one sidewalk and down the other, stopping in no less than five sweatshirt shops before he found *the one*. I mean, admittedly, it was a pretty kick-butt hoodie. Or pullover. It had this ombre effect to make it look like the sky turning from dusk to night.

For mine, I picked a pretty lavender with white lettering. Both of ours had a picture of the bridge drawn and said Mackinaw City. But mine had the added design detail of a v-neckline instead of the traditional scoop and had fake lamb's wool on the inside for extra insulation.

That done, I dragged him to the pancake house that I remembered eating at as a kid.

And this really was why we clicked so well, when I couldn't decide between two specialty pancakes, Len ordered one and had me order the other (along with sausage and bacon for us to share) and when it came to the table, he split them between the two of us.

"Best of both worlds," he said.

Major crush overload.

He switched the last two missions. We found a fudge shop that smelled too good to walk away from first after spending some time walking down by the water's edge and snapping pictures of the lighthouse and the bridge.

Our last *mission* stop, we hit up a coffee shop. Our last *stop* stop he filled up the gas tank and then climbed back inside the truck to start our trek over the lakes.

"Take the singing bridge side?" I asked.

"Was hoping you'd say that," he said. "It's one of my favorite parts."

What made the bridge sing were the grates instead of pavement. That allowed the wind to move through so the road didn't crack. You could see the water down below. It was so cool, but some people got scared and preferred the paved side.

I videoed us going up and over. For people who hadn't been, it was hard to describe how breathtakingly beautiful the view. Once we reached the other side, we stopped at the toll to pay and continued on through. St. Ignace, the first city we traveled through on our way inland, owned the distinction of being the second oldest European settled city in Michigan.

That fact fascinated me for some reason.

The change in the land from one side of the straights to

the other came on immediately. From rolling hills, maples, and birch to rocky terrain with conifers like spruce.

"Keep your eye out for a moose," I said.

"Say again?"

"A moose. They have them up here and I want to see one. So keep your eyes open."

"Who's my fearless girl, wanting to see wild animals."

"Not wild animals, just a moose. It's not like I'm actively seeking out a mountain lion."

"Would you prefer I not point out a mountain lion if I see one?"

I thought about it. "Well, no. If you see a mountain lion, you're morally obliged to point it out."

"Right. Look for moose. Point out mountain lions. Anything else?"

"Well... if you're going to point out a lion, you might as well point out a bear. Or a wolf."

"Got it," he said. "Oh, if you see a deer, point it out for me, okay?"

"Um... sure. But we have deer back home."

"Yeah, I know. I don't want to hit one there either."

Cheeky.

Well, as it turned out, we didn't see any cool wild animals. Actually, the only ones we saw were mangled remains of roadkill. Some deer carcasses, but mostly that of racoons, skunk, muskrat, and opossums.

Long stretches of barren land on each side of us made me think that there'd been a pretty significant forest fire not too far in the past. Maybe a couple of years judging from the new growth.

It was getting late by the time we hit the outskirts of Marquette county. Up here, late meant dark. Way dark.

Len decided to find us a hotel for the night and we'd set off for our camping adventure in the morning.

What a difference it made to hit the city of Marquette. Lights lit up the front of us, while blackness swallowed up the road behind. Marquette, being home to a pretty large university, had everything anyone would need, but with that downhome feel from being tucked away in crook of Lake Superior's shoreline.

He found us a nice hotel and checked us in. I didn't want to retire to our room just yet. We walked around. Took in the remains of a festival happening down by the marina, then walked to dinner.

We stopped at a delicious little sushi joint. Yes, I know, sushi in the upper peninsula of Michigan? Well, Lake Superior had lots of fish and even if they flew it in frozen, it tasted freaking fantastic.

After dinner, we strolled to a little bar that was having an open mic night. I sipped on a rum and diet coke while he drank a beer. Three singers later, we decided to check out the other nightlife, eventually making our way into a dive where a spoken-word poetry contest put on by the university was being held. Len and I stayed to the end of the contest to see who'd been picked the winner—a woman who used a sinking ship as a metaphor for her life after she started seeing her boyfriend, who'd turned violently abusive.

She deserved to win for what she'd lived through, though she was also the best in my opinion, and that was saying something.

After, with his arm slung around my waist, and my head on his shoulder, we slowly made our way back to the hotel, where I may or may not have gotten a little frisky with Len.

And may or may not have taken advantage of him orally while he returned the favor.

Our intensions of getting up bright and early went out the window as we stayed up later than intended—*eh-hem*—entertaining each other and thus checkout happened at about eleven. Still, we had plenty of time to drive up into the mountains and find our camping spot.

Len pretty well knew where he wanted us to go. I forgot Michigan had mountains, living my life in the lower peninsula. Sure, they weren't as tall as those out west or down south, but they were still good-sized mountains.

Today I wore socks and hiking boots. Good thing, as there came a point where he had to park the truck because he couldn't drive any farther. We loaded up our backpacks and this little camping wagon with a handle that hooked around Len's waist so he could pull it behind him. The wheels, big enough to move easily over mountain terrain, made hiking with camping gear a piece of cake. At least Len made it look like a piece of cake.

Before we left, he wrote on a piece of paper: *Camping. Truck not abandoned.*

He stuck the paper in the front window for anyone who came upon the truck to read. He bleeped the locks and then we hiked.

As a jump instructor, Len kept one of those go-cameras strapped to a helmet in the backseat, so he could record the jumps for his clients. He fastened the helmet to his head and I couldn't help but giggle. He kind of looked ridiculous hiking with a helmet cam on his head.

Normally, he used his phone, but I understood why this would be more convenient.

I guess I never realized how long it took to hike up a mountain. Hours we spent searching out the perfect camping spot, finally reaching a plateau clear enough to set up the tent. And his tent, it set itself up. Literally, it unfolded on its own into a dome once we pulled it from the thin, cylindrical bag. Refolding it would be the work.

"Well, that went easy enough," I said.

He shoved my shoulder lightly. "Yeah... yeah."

I didn't understand what he meant by the playful gesture. "It didn't?" I asked.

His face dropped to a stone-cold serious expression. "Oh, you were serious."

"Yes... did I say something wrong?"

Len bent over and started clearing a spot close to the tent—but not too close—of debris such as leaves and sticks and twigs. "We have to make a firepit for warmth and protection that won't burn down the forest."

Of course, a fire pit. Didn't I feel stupid? "What do you need me to do?"

"This is a natural place to camp, so it looks like people have made our job a bit easier." With the last few leaves, sticks, and pieces of trash out of the way, a dirt circle surrounded by stones revealed itself. "See these stones, they're the barrier. We just have to reinforce them and gather firewood.

"That makes sense," I said. "It's just... I've never camped before. Roughing it for us as kids meant staying at my grandmother's cabin. We never slept in tents and her firepit had been purchased from a home goods store."

I thought he'd make at least a little bit of fun of me for being a priss, but he didn't. "No, I get it. Not everyone's family camps. Mine didn't either after my parents' divorce. Mom never wanted to do any activities that reminded her of Dad. Now my brother and I would go every summer. Just he and I. It was our chance to catch up."

"Catch up?" I asked.

Len stood on the end of one of the thicker sticks—one might even call it a thin tree branch—and pulled up to break it in half. He did this several more times to several more sticks, then stacked them once he had enough, stuffing dried leaves and a paper cup that other campers had left behind into open spots between the sticks for kindling. Even I knew that much.

Just because my grandmother's firepit came from a box didn't mean she'd neglected to teach me how to start a fire.

"He told the judge that he wanted to live with my dad, thinking they'd give me the same choice." He shrugged. "But I was four years younger and never got asked. My parents decided if he was staying with Dad, then I'd get sent to live with Mom."

Before he finished telling his story, a brilliant fire blazed in the pit. We'd have to hunt up more wood to keep it going, but at least we had a start and I could whip us up something to eat.

I wanted to ask him more about his brother, but his whole demeanor changed. He seemed sad and we weren't about sad, not today. That decided, I asked, what did we pack to eat?"

"I have steaks in the cooler." Lifting his finger and thumb in the shape of a gun, he flicked his wrist as if taking a shot, the '*gun*' pointed at the cart, and he made a clicking noise with his mouth.

"How do you eat your steaks?" I asked.

Len stretched his arms up over his head, lifting the bottom of his T-shirt to show a strip of golden tanned skin. "With a knife and fork," he said, winking at me.

"So well done it is," I teased back. I'd sooner bite a cow's behind than condemn a beautiful sirloin to end its days as a dried-out piece of charcoal.

The grimace he sent me was exactly the reaction I wanted.

Point for Kami. *Yes.*

TWELVE

It had been an amazing night. Just Len and I. The weather, perfect. Warm with a slight breeze. While I fixed dinner, he gathered more branches that were close by. Then after dinner, we went on a broader search together.

Once it started to get dark, he broke out the marshmallows, chocolate squares, and graham crackers for s'mores. I hadn't eaten s'mores in years. And there was just something about eating sweets under the stars. In our little clearing, the canopy of trees opened up enough for us to see thousands of them. A star-studded extravaganza.

When we decided to retire to the tent, Len took our separate sleeping bags and zipped them together into one big sleeping bag.

I undressed down to my skivvies. As did Len. It wasn't guaranteed, but I figured some sexy times might take place. We managed some canoodling—touching, kissing, and whatnots—but it appeared we'd both been too worn out from all the hiking and firewood scavenging to do much more. We actually passed out in each other's arms pretty quickly.

The next morning, we dressed. "We're going hiking," he said.

Len got the coffee going, along with the eggs and bacon he'd so smartly packed in the—*I kid not*—generator operated cooler before we left home, while I prettied myself up. Yes, we were out in the middle of nowhere, but I still had a gorgeous fake boyfriend to try and keep for as long as I could keep him. And wrinkles waited for no woman. Even we young ones could expect them to creep over our faces if we didn't take precautions. Thus, I slathered cream over my skin.

The beautiful man known as Len handed me off a cup of coffee when I screwed the last cap back on the last of my bottles. We sipped from our mugs and then when they were finished cooking, we sipped from our mugs and ate.

We made sure the fire was completely out before we set off. I used a tub to wash the dishes, then dumped the water onto the embers.

Thick brush turned thicker the farther up the mountain we hiked. It wasn't like we hiked the Sierra Madres or Rockies, but for a girl who never hiked up anything until recently, I began wheezing when the incline took a steep turn.

Being the perfect gentleman guide, he stopped for me every time (and there were a lot of times) I needed to stop. He paid enough attention that I didn't even have to say anything. Though I supposed breathing so heavy it sounded like a chainsaw buzzing while leaning against a tree for support might have been a good indicator. Full disclosure: I didn't sound like a chainsaw buzzing. That was an exaggeration. I did, however, stop on several occasions to rest.

Several hours later—yes, my frequent breaks added a whole lot of time to our trek—with sweat-glistened skin, we reached the summit. Breathtaking. Of course, it would be even more beautiful out west, but we weren't out west, and I couldn't think of a more beautiful sight in the whole of Michigan.

We turned around to take a selfie with the vista behind us. Len and I at the top of our world. Not *the* world, as there were summits far greater. Baby steps. I'd take *our world* for now. Happy with the pictures, we turned back to take in the view once again. I felt small and insignificant staring out at the wide, wide wilderness. As it was cooler from the altitude, the sweat on my skin didn't just cool, but chilled me.

Still, I couldn't get myself to leave.

The loose rock underfoot held different ideas. One tiny pivot to take another gander at the gorgeous man standing next to me and his reaction to the beauty set before us. That was all it took. My foot slipped and I flailed my arms in an attempt to catch my balance. It didn't work. My other foot slipped right out from underneath me, sending me sliding down over the side of the rocky surface.

Scratches scraped across my skin, gashes opening up. Those stung, but if I kept sliding, stinging wouldn't matter. Not on this stretch of mountain. This rock laid flat enough to let me slide right off the side.

My life—well, not really my whole life—but my regrets passed in front of my eyes. That night I'd made a pass at Harrison. The catalyst for every bad thing to follow occupied most of my thoughts in those few seconds before I plunged over the side to certain death.

I think I might have heard Len screaming. But with a head filled with regrets, including not getting the chance to see how long I could stretch this thing with Len, it was hard to focus on anything else.

Dirt and rocks caked under my fingernails as I tried

futilely to slow the short descent. My hips slid over the side when a hand gripped my upper arm. My body wanted to keep falling and it felt like my shoulder popped out of joint.

That didn't matter either. Len had lunged for me, landing on his belly. The top-half of his torso bent over the ledge. One strong hand separated me from death. I didn't want to die. The strain on his face said everything. He might have had me now—and I wasn't going to be confused with a beached whale anytime soon—but with my weight and the slope of the rock, his hand started slipping.

His toes hooked under a thin rim of rock, the only thing keeping us alive, or at least me alive. The muscles of his calves contracted to the point they vibrated. His whole body went taut under the strain. And then we locked eyes.

"I got you, baby. I'm not letting go," he said. I think he tried to convince himself, more than for my benefit.

I couldn't speak. Tears choked off any words.

He started to pull. As my legs dangled, I had nothing to help push. The strain and fatigue on his face was evident. But he kept pulling in a solitary effort until my thighs cleared the rock and I could bend my knees. Then I was able to gain enough traction to push. Len wiggled his body to move backward. Slowly, together, we moved me back up the rock until I hit safety.

Len saved my life.

He *saved* my life.

I burst out in a fit of wails and tears. Clutching Len's T-shirt, I buried my face against his chest. His arms wrapped tightly around me.

"Sh—*hiccup*—shh..." He hiccupped.

My gaze found his. Red-rimmed, tear-filled eyes. That made me cry even harder. Something about seeing a guy cry got me in the feels.

Once we were both together enough to stand, he helped me up. My arm hurt like a son of a gun. I just knew my shoulder was dislocated now. And as for those big gashes, which still bled quasi-profusely, well, with my nerves continuing to heighten from my near death, the stinging became profound.

He cleared his throat. "I've got some bandages in the backpack. Let me wrap that gash." He pulled a roll of bandages, medical tape, and peroxide from the backpack he wore. He poured the peroxide over all my cuts and scrapes and then wrapped my wounds until my leg looked like a mummy.

Still, my shoulder kept me from being able to move. I hated being so weak. We had to go, so I swallowed hard and pushed past the pain. Leaning against him, we hobbled slowly back down the mountain. Every movement made me wince. But I thought I hid it pretty well.

It was dark by the time we found the campsite. Len had to use a flashlight to guide our way for like half the journey. By the time he set me down close to the firepit, I felt like I was going to puke. Pain. Who knew it could cause such a reaction?

As Len started building a fire, I bent over and puked. Or I tried to puke. Nothing really came up. But that man was back at my side in an instant.

"What's wrong?" he asked.

Part of me wanted to blow it off, keep him from worrying. Yet I couldn't lie. Not to Len. He'd saved my life. "I dislocated my shoulder," I admitted.

His eyes grew huge as a scowl spread across his lips. "Baby, why didn't you tell me?"

"I didn't want you to worry."

"You've been dealing with a dislocation this whole

time? Kam, I know how to pop it back. With the jobs I do, I had to take triage training."

Why didn't I think of that? Oh yeah, because I'd almost died and I'd been in pain ever since.

"I didn't think of that," I said.

A soft chuckle escaped him. From the harrowing experience up at the summit, we'd gotten back to the point where he could chuckle. Sneaky. I'd gotten so lost in his chuckle that I neglected to notice him position himself to my opposite shoulder.

"Ready?" he asked.

I nodded. Now or never.

He wrapped himself around me, hands locked at my armpit, and the best I can describe it, it sort of looked like an intense Heimlich maneuver. In and up in one smooth motion. It hurt so much worse.

Two tries, we actually heard it pop back into place. I felt it pop. The pain fled as soon as joint found socket. Instantaneously. Sure, it stayed sore, but I'd take sore over outright pain any day of the week.

He kissed me then. Not one of his lust-filled Len kisses —well, okay, not *totally* one of his lust-filled Len kisses— there was relief mixed in there. I detected warmth, too.

Just as quickly as he swept me up, he abruptly let me go. "Fire," he said and set about finishing getting the fire going. He placed a pot real close, close enough for it to heat up hot. Then he opened two cans of beef stew and dumped them in the pot, along with a can of peas, corn, and carrots. He even added seasoning from a seasoning mix he'd brought. The man seriously thought of everything. Really, how had he managed to pack all this with an hour of prep time before we'd left?

Ten minutes passed before I sat, my leg stretched out in

front of me, with a bowl of stew on my lap. Len tore off three soft rolls from the package and handed two of them to me. One he dropped in his bowl so he could tear himself off a second.

In relative silence, *companionable* silence, we ate our supper. He twisted off the cap of a dark stout beer for himself but handed me a pineapple cider instead. Bellies full, he cleaned up the dinner and lay down with his arms folded behind his head as a makeshift pillow. I lay down next to him.

"Thank you," I said. "You saved my life today."

"I thought I was going to lose you, honestly." A soft breath of air left his nose. "I'd never been so scared in my entire life."

"Join the club."

"Don't ever do that to me again, Kam."

My back went taut, the lightness leaving my words. "It's not like I did it on purpose. There were loose rocks. I slipped. It was an accident."

"I know, jeepus, I know. How would you expect me to go on?"

"It'd be tough, but as it wasn't your fault, you'd find a way."

"I'd find a way," he muttered. "Right. Just don't do it again."

I knew it was still his fear talking, so instead of arguing, I agreed. "Okay, Len. I won't do it again."

"Woman, you are so going to be the death of *me*."

As I didn't understand what he meant by that, I ignored it. I think both of us wanted to partake in some post-'*I almost died*' nookie, but my injuries kept him from acting on his urges.

Len gave my wounds a thorough looking over when he

changed the wrap to apply antibiotic spray. Consensus: I wouldn't need stitches. The gashes scabbed over nicely.

Since I continued to heal, I managed to talk him out of us leaving so soon. As long as no infection set in, why not stay? I had ibuprofen in my purse for any lingering pain. Len took it upon himself to make sure infection wouldn't worm its way in. And honestly, being up here away from civilization, every moment getting to know Len more, at least the things he was willing to talk about meant a lot to me. The man was seriously guarded when it came to talking about his brother. That was a conversation ender, so I stayed safely away from that topic. It came at a great cost to my heart. I would whittle him down, though. Eventually he'd spill his guts and smile while doing it. At least I hoped he would.

The problem with so much one-on-one time, though, was that I came to the realization at the end of the week when we started packing up our campsite that my serious crush had taken a bad, bad turn.

Somehow, well, I'd managed to let myself fall—I mean it wasn't that hard. He was a great guy, treated me like I mattered—I'd fallen pretty hard for Len.

Spending almost half a month with someone continuously at your side, these things happened. How did I expect to make it through our six months abroad now? Watching him woo other women with a screaming crush would've been bad enough. But doing it in love with the guy? In unrequited love with the guy?

"You truly are fearless, Kams," he said, packing up the last of our gear we'd hiked down to the truck. "You almost died, yet stayed up on that mountain with me. I'm so proud of you."

His words felt more profound for me now and my skin

blushed from the compliment. "I love—" I gasped. What did I almost say?

"What?" he asked.

"I was going to say that I actually love camping." I covered. *Phew*. "Never thought I would, but up here, despite the nearly fatal mishap, I loved it."

"Yeah, *despite* that."

THIRTEEN

Ten hours after we left the mountain (we stopped to eat, stretch our legs, and take pictures) we turned into his parking spot in front of the condo. To say I was whipped would be an understatement.

There'd be time to unpack the truck tomorrow. For now, we both needed a shower and to veg out with a movie until we passed out.

Exactly what we did. But not before Len uploaded our entire trip to my social media accounts. After all, we'd kept radio silence for a week.

At the end of a third round of morning nookie, my cell rang. My mom.

"Hey, Mom, what's up?"

"Sweetie, I've been trying to get ahold of you."

"Sorry, I went camping and we were in the middle of nowhere. No cell reception." That was the honest truth.

"It's your father," she said. Her voice cracked.

My breath left my lungs.

I swallowed. "Is he... *okay?*"

"Yes, I mean, no. Yes and no. He had a small heart

attack. He's in the hospital. They're putting a stent in his artery today."

"When?"

"At four."

I gripped Len's hand and squeezed.

"Kam, baby, what's wrong?" he asked in one ear.

While my mom asked, "Who's that?" in the other.

"He's my—*um*—Len." I didn't want to lie to her and say he was my boyfriend, but I didn't want to admit he was fake either.

"Can you come home, Kami? I need you," Mom said, as if I wouldn't be showering and rushing out the door as soon as I got her off the phone.

"Of course I'm coming, Mom. What kind of daughter do you think I am?"

"The best kind," she said. "Love you sweetheart."

"Love you too, Mom." I disconnected and stood from the bed naked and uncaring. He'd seen it all numerous times.

"Is everything okay?" Len asked. "Your mom okay?"

I nodded. "It's my dad—he had a heart attack. He's having surgery today. She'd like me there."

Len shot up from the bed. "Then let's get ready." He started pulling clean clothes from the drawers, tossing them into my overnight bag he rescued from the closet. Then, to my surprise, he started piling his clothes on top of mine.

"What are you doing?" I asked.

"Baby, shower," he said.

"I'm going... but what are you—?"

"You think I'm going to leave you in the lurch when your dad is sick? Give me some credit. That doesn't make me much of a boyfriend, now does it?"

"Well, no, not if you were real, but we're—"

He cut me off again. "Kam, wake up. We've *never* been fake. I liked you for a long time, wanted to get to know you. So, when you gave me my opening, I took it."

"You? We? We've never been fake?"

The next thing I knew, Len's arms wrapped tightly around my waist, drawing me in close. Then he kissed me. Hard and deep and sweet. A real boyfriend kiss. Because apparently, he'd been my real boyfriend all this time?

"Never been fake," he answered.

"Then why did you let me think it for so long?"

"Well, to be honest, I thought you'd catch on by now. I'll give you anything you need, baby. If that means letting you pretend we're fake for a while..." He shrugged.

"So you're coming home with me?"

Instead of answering, he kissed me a second time, then swatted my butt to get me moving. I showered, then while I dressed, he did. All our camping gear still in the bed of the truck, we headed to my childhood home.

I loved my family, but it was hard to go back, to be there without my brother, so I rarely did. My folks understood. With Len to hold my hand when the memories got rough, I might be able to handle it this time.

At the end of a two-and-a-half-hour drive, we pulled into the parking garage at the hospital. My mom texted me she was in my dad's room. She tacked on his *"Looking forward to seeing you, kiddo. xo"* at the end. Took more than a heart attack and impending surgery to keep my dad down.

Since in her text Mom had already told us which floor and room to find them in, we bypassed the help desk, walking straight for the elevators. With the hospital complex being so huge, we had to find the right bank of elevators first.

My mother's face completely lit up when Len and I

walked into the room. She jumped from her chair next to my dad's bed, tears overflowing her worried blue eyes, and ran to embrace me. She hugged and hugged.

"Missed you, Mom," I said.

"I missed you, too, sweetheart."

Dad cleared his throat. Admittedly, not as strongly as he'd have cleared it before, which sent a jolt of worry to my gut.

"Hey, Dad." I released my mom and walked over. Bending down, I kissed his cheek.

"What? No hug for your old man?"

"I didn't want to..." My intensions mattered not. That was Dad's way of saying he wanted a hug and I dang-well better give him one. So I bent in and as softly as I could, hugged my dad.

"Good to see you, kiddo," he whispered in my ear. Then he turned to look at Len. "Now, who is this gentleman who escorted my daughter up here?"

Len walked up to my dad's bed, hand outstretched. "I'm Len, Kam's boyfriend."

"Kami," my father chided, "why didn't you tell us you hooked yourself a man?"

"Because I was worried you'd say something like 'I hooked myself a man.' Imagine my chagrin." I said, *hooked myself a man* in my stickiest sweet Scarlett O'Hara impression.

Dad laughed until his laugh turned to coughing. The nurse heard and popped her head inside the room. "Do not rile him up."

Ouch. Scolded by the nurse.

Mom, Len, and I held in our laughs until she disappeared out the door again, then we lost it.

"Well, you certainly are easy on the eyes, Len," my mom said.

"*Mom*," I protested.

"What? He is. And I'm sure it's not something he doesn't already know."

"Then you don't need to remind him."

"Oh, I don't mind being reminded," Len said through his snicker. "My own girlfriend doesn't tell me she finds me attractive, so..."

I punched him. Just in the shoulder and it clearly didn't hurt him. But I had to prove a point. A silent point. That being, up until this morning, I'd thought he was my fake boyfriend and thus it would've been inappropriate for me to call him attractive.

Yes, I figured all that could be conveyed through a punch. For good measure, I threw in, "And you *are* super hot."

My mother invited us to sit down, so Len and I sat on the two-person beige vinyl loveseat in between her chair and my dad in the bed. As we talked, Dad kept looking over at Len. He'd cock his head and squint his eyes, as if concentrating, then after a few seconds, he'd shake his head and try to rejoin the conversation.

The third time of him doing this, my father finally asked, "Do I know you from somewhere, Len?"

Len started and a strange expression crossed his face, but it withered away to be replaced by a genuine smile. "No. I just have one of those faces. People always think they know me from somewhere or other." He waved off the comment with a flick of his hand.

In the background, the beeping machine keeping track of my dad's heartbeats, blood pressure, and all that other stuff I didn't fully understand, became the fifth member to our party. My dad looked so frail in that bed, his color pale instead of rosy. The wrinkles seemed more prominent. As did the gray in his hair and beard. Dad never looked his age, and now he didn't just not look his age, but he looked several years older. At least a decade.

Tears welled in my eyes. I wouldn't cry, at least not in front of him. Not without knowing how my tears would affect him. Len looked at me, then reached over to take my hand in his. The gentle squeeze helped more than he'd ever know. It was funny. We'd been together such a short time— wow, how weird to think we were actually together? All that time I'd thought we were playing—and he knew me, knew when I needed that added support.

A knock sounded on the door and the nurse poked her head in. "It's time," she said as she pushed the door all the way open. Two nursing assistants accompanied her. A woman pushing the gurney and a man walking along next to the woman pushing the gurney.

Worry flashed in my dad's eyes. I couldn't blame him. We all worried. Sure, heart surgeons put stents in clogged arteries all the time, but it was still a major surgery.

My mother attempted to stifle a sob unsuccessfully. My dad, to his credit, lifted his hand to grasp my mom's. He brought it slowly, while wincing, up to his lips to kiss her knuckles.

"I can't lose you," she said to him. "I can't. I buried my boy..." Mom's lips quivered as the tears flowed freely.

I didn't want to leave, but at the same time it felt like an invasion of their privacy. This was a moment meant for a long-married couple and not for anyone else's ears or eyes.

Totally oblivious to the moment my parents were having, the nurse broke in. "We'll take good care of him."

Though I supposed a huge deal for us was simply business as usual for them. The female assistant locked the wheels of the gurney next to my dad's bed and the three of them transferred him. Next, the guardrails went up and locked in place. At that point they let us get close to Dad before they took him away.

I bent in and kissed his cheek, dampening both our cheeks from crying. "Love you, old man."

Once I moved out of the way, Len stepped up. He patted my dad on the shoulder. "Sorry to have our first meeting be under these circumstances. I'll be thinking good thoughts."

"Thank you, son. For what it's worth, I'm glad I got to meet you." Dad took a second to catch his breath. "It's a lot to ask of a man you just met, but I'm asking anyway. Take care of my girls. They're sensitive and will need a strong shoulder to cry on while their waiting on me to recover."

"You have my word, sir." Len gave that same shoulder a squeeze. "Take care," he said, then stepped back.

At that point, we both let my mom have her moment with him without listening in. At first his arm slid around my shoulders, but when they pushed the gurney out of the room, my mother walking with them holding my dad's hand, Len turned me into him so he could full-on hug me. I never appreciated his strong arms as much as I did at that moment.

Brian had been great after my brother passed. We'd only been dating six months when it happened. Then with all the stalking and harassment that followed from Leo, Harrison's brother, and I had to move, he moved too—gave up a job and everything. Albeit, a crappy minimum wage job that he didn't mind leaving as it provided him the opportunity to find a much better one in the field he wanted to work in. But he did it for no other reason than so we wouldn't be apart.

Len's hug felt like an absorption of everything. My dad's surgery. Losing my brother. Leo. And even Brian. The man clearly had no clue what he was getting himself into when he'd decided to date me for real.

The staff allowed us to stay in the room because it had been assigned to my dad and they'd be bringing him back here after his stint in recovery. Mom appeared in the doorway, bottom lip quivering, but she stayed strong. Too strong for the situation, in my opinion.

"Mom, have you eaten today?" I got to her side in only a couple of steps.

But she moved past me to sit down in the chair next to the empty bed. "I'm not hungry."

"How are you gonna take care of Dad if you aren't taking care of yourself? Please, let me get you some soup or something."

"Okay, sweetheart. I'll eat some soup." She agreed far too easily.

I beckoned Len over with my finger. As he reached me, I pulled him in to a private conversation. "She needs to eat. Can you sit with her while I go?"

"You want me to go, baby?"

Shaking my head *no*, I used my eyes to gesture for him to look at her. "Her husband went to surgery and she's not crying. That's not right. She's being strong for me. You stay, please. Give her a safe place to let go."

"If that's what you want."

My hand to the back of his neck, I pulled him in for a kiss. "Thank you, Len. I'll grab you something too, okay?"

A second kiss, this one from Len, and he let me go. Out of the corner of my eye, I watched him take a seat on the edge of the bed and pull my mom in for a hug. What I told him was true. She wouldn't let go with me in the room. But what I neglected to mention was that I needed the space. So many emotions swirling around inside one little body.

I worried for my dad. The guilt I felt for staying away was probably giving me an ulcer as I walked to the elevator. Not to mention I'd fallen in love with Len and couldn't bring myself to tell him because *hello?* Chicken.

My phone picked that time to ping with another email. I pulled it from my pocket. Brian. Why wouldn't he leave me alone? We'd broken up. He'd broken up with me. He'd just gotten engaged to another woman.

Well, Brian happened to be one thing I could avoid dealing with for the time being. Yet again, I swiped to delete his message just as I reached the elevators. One was just about to close when I threw my hand between to stop it. The doors pulled back open to the empty elevator car. I pressed and held the *door close* button just to make sure I didn't have to share the ride with anyone.

On the first floor, I followed the smell of food to the cafeteria. Along with the regular cafeteria fare of burgers, pizza, fries, etc., they offered a spread of pretty credible Chinese food. I got mom a pint of the wonton soup. For me and Len, the Lo Mein noodles. And for all of us to share, fried pork wontons, crab-cheese rangoons, and eggrolls. What better for people waiting on a heart patient having a stent put in his clogged artery to eat than fried foods?

Some days comfort outweighed practicality. Today comfort won out.

FOURTEEN

Back on my dad's floor, I walked into the room in time to see my mom throw her head back and laugh. That man had magic in his blood. I knew it had been the right choice to have him stay, and I'm so glad he agreed with me. I'd never have gotten her to laugh.

"Hey there," I said.

Both heads turned to look at me. "A mud slip-n-slide, sweetheart?" My mom asked, what I believed to be rhetorically, so I didn't answer.

Instead I shot *what-the-heck-did-you-say-to-her* eyes to my soon-to-be-ex boyfriend if he didn't give the answer I wanted.

"What?" he asked. "She wanted to know how we met. Then she wanted to know how we'd gotten together. Was I supposed to lie?"

"Yes. You were supposed to tell her we met at a church social or at a homeless shelter or volunteering at a no-kill animal shelter."

"Like I'd believe you went to church socials?" my mom quipped.

"You're only supposed to believe good things about me —like I was kissed by angels or fairies fly out of my butt... I don't know."

"Fairies?" Mom laughed again. "That would probably hurt."

"No wonder my brother—" Len started to say, but then stopped himself.

"Your brother?" Mom asked.

He shook his head. "He used to say, 'Look at how a girl interacts with her family to know if you need to stick around.'"

"And do you need to stick around?" she asked then.

"Foods getting cold." I cut in before he had the chance to answer, holding up the tray.

He smirked but stood and grabbed the soup to hand to my mom. We spread the rest of the cartons on the small table. Mom's eyes got huge when she spied my noodles.

"Is that Lo Mein?" she asked, like she couldn't tell.

"Yup," I answered and made a big show of sticking my chopsticks in the container to pull out what turned out to be a mouthful of delicious, saucy delightfulness. I slurped the noodles, flicking sauce all over my lips and cheeks. "Mmm..." I finished dramatically.

Mom looked between her soup and my Lo Mein several times. I was going to have to force-feed her when I'd left and now she wanted my food? My meal enjoyment just cut itself by half.

"Huh." She sighed. "You give birth to children and raise them the best you can. Give up everything for their comfort... This one"—she pointed to me—"I was in labor with her for thirty-nine hours before they finally had to cut me open for a C-section."

I couldn't take it anymore. "Here, Mom." I handed her over the container of noodles.

"No, I couldn't." Oh, she said she couldn't as she snatched the carton from my hand and dug in with her own set of chopsticks that I'd brought her in case she wanted to try the fried pork wontons.

The wonton soup tasted delicious, but I wanted what I'd ordered.

To my utter surprise, Len reached over and grabbed the soup from my hands. "Share with me?" he asked.

My mouth dropped open as I stared at him for a beat.

"What?" he asked. "It smells good. We share, we get the best of both."

"Best of both," I repeated dumbly, then snapped my mouth closed and picked up a rangoon.

Eventually, well after we'd finished eating, we got word that Dad was out of surgery and they'd moved him to recovery. He'd done well and everything looked good.

Dad acted pretty groggy when they finally wheeled him back into the room. He looked at Len and said, "Do I know you?"

That's when Mom stepped in and said, "That's Len, honey. You met him earlier."

Dad nodded slightly and then passed out again. He still had a lot of the anesthesia in his system.

Eventually, we had to leave for the night. Mom and I kissed Dad while Len gave his arm a quick squeeze, exactly as he had before my dad had left for his surgery.

The drive back to my childhood home went quickly yet quietly. The stresses of the day sort of caught up with us all. Mom let us in. Len carried our bags.

"I'm awfully tired," she said. "Think I'll head to bed."

She kissed my cheek first, and then went up on her tiptoes to kiss Len's.

When she was gone down the hall Len turned to me. "Am I allowed to share a room with you? Or do I take the couch?"

"You can have the couch if you want it, but I'm sure my parents hold no pretense that you aren't screwing my brains out on a nightly basis."

"It's not *nightly*."

"I know that, but we're young. They think everyone our age screws nightly."

"*Ouch*," Len said, laughing. "Your poor vagina. Maybe give a girl some recover time."

"That's what I'm saying."

"Makes me wonder about your parents."

"Don't." I put my hand up. "Don't even go there."

Grabbing his hand, I tugged him halfway down the hall to my old bedroom, now turned guest room.

We stripped down and changed into our pajamas, took turns using the bathroom, and climbed into bed. As soon as my head hit the pillow... nothing. I couldn't turn my brain off. I lay on a bent arm facing Len. He took on the exact same pose, facing me.

"How are you doing?" he asked.

"Better, knowing Dad'll be okay. Thank you for this, today. Coming. I didn't even realize how much I needed you here until you were here."

"Sort of comes with the boyfriend job description. But you're welcome. I'd have gone crazy not knowing how you were doing."

He leaned in to kiss me and right as his lips touched mine, I asked, "How come you always stop yourself when you talk about your brother?"

Probably not the best time to have asked that, seeing as Len rolled back over to his original spot. "It's hard. We were... *close*. But like you, my brother died. I didn't handle it well. Actually, I sort of went off the rails on a crazy train. It got pretty bad. So I just don't like thinking about it. Thinking about him makes me think of the stuff I did."

"And you can't separate the two? The memories of your brother from the crazy stuff you did?"

"I hurt some people in my grief. Not physically, but I'm really not proud of that."

"Have you tried to apologize?" I asked.

His stare drilled into me. I'd never felt anything more intense. "Kami, baby, I'm going to kiss you now."

And he did. He rolled over me, pinning me to the bed, and took my lips in possibly the hottest make-out session we'd ever had. I squirmed underneath him as I groped his backside. But right when I was about to hit pay dirt, he moved my hand and rolled away, leaving me a heavily panting, confused mess.

"Wha?" Yes, the panting continued so hard, I couldn't even finish the word.

"I'm not having sex with you here. Your mom is two doors down."

"But," I whined. Not my proudest moment, but I *really* wanted to have sex. Now.

"When we get home, baby. You can have me every way you want me. Just not here, not tonight."

It felt like there was something else going on here, more than him not wanting sex because of my mom, but I didn't push it. If he needed us to wait, we'd wait.

"Hold me?" I asked.

Len laid me out with a sweet caress of his lips this time. "That I can do."

Dad was released the next afternoon and Len and I decided to wait the rest of the week to go home. Not a man to stay idle, Len mowed the grass, then changed the oil in my mom's car because Dad had recently done his but had the heart attack before he'd gotten to Mom's. Len generally did any fix-it things on the to-do list my parents kept tacked to the refrigerator. He'd come in, check one off, and then head back out to tackle another one.

My dad could've gone back to work after a few days, but my mom made him take vacation time while Len and I visited. Mostly, I think, because she worried. My parents were only in their early fifties. Much too young to be dealing with heart attacks and blocked arteries. The problem probably occurred because dear old Dad, though he wasn't overweight, never in all my years of knowing him let "that green stuff" touch his plate.

I ate vegetables. Len ate vegetables. *Mom* ate vegetables. How a man went his whole life not eating them went beyond my comprehension. They bickered back and forth. He ate potatoes, that counted. That didn't count.

Mom was right, but I stayed out of their tiffs.

By the end of the week, with Dad doing well, family time got to be too much. Especially after I informed them that I'd be setting sail with Len and the Lowenstein's for half a year. They had some choice words for me. For Len. For Dion. But in the end begrudgingly gave their okay, not that I needed it. Things between us became somewhat stained after that. So we decided to head home. Plus, you know, I wanted me some Len booty—*bad*.

We packed up, I kissed my parents goodbye and promised not to stay away so long again. Well, after we got back from sailing around the world, that is. Mom made Len promise to come back with me.

"She wants me, I'm there," he said.

Then we climbed in the truck and drove away. Out of the side mirror, I watched them wave to us.

Len grasped my hand in his and brought them both to rest on his knee. A coffee stop, a pee break, and two and a half hours of drive time, we made it back home safely.

Home. Len's place? Our place? What was the dynamic now that we were an actual couple? It was far too soon to "*move in together*," but essentially, we had. And being on a boat for six months, unless we broke up, we would probably continue to share a bed.

After bringing our stuff from this week into the house, I started up a load of laundry while Len unloaded the truck bed of the gear we'd brought camping the week before. When he walked in, the last load having been stored away in his storage unit, the sun hit behind him, glistening around him to the point he had this golden-white aura, my breath caught in my throat. I swallowed hard.

Unsure of what to say, because he caught me staring hard, I asked, "Can I cut your hair?"

He nodded.

I pulled out the barstool and motioned for him to sit down. Then I went to the bedroom to retrieve my box of goodies—comb, scissors, spray bottle—that I'd brought with me when I left the salon. As I walked back down the hallway, I grabbed a towel from the linen closet.

With the towel draped around his shoulders, he sat for me. I picked up the spray bottle to spritz his hair, dampening all the strands. I looked over his face shape, found the way his hair naturally fell, and gathered up a thick bunch between my fingers. Something changed in the room as I snipped. The air felt thick, heavy. Every breath weighty.

Why? I had no idea. But as the hair drifted to the floor,

his intense stare never left me. It touched me physically. Or that was how it felt. When I finished, I pulled at the hairs by his temples to make sure they were even. He stayed my hand, gently forcing the scissors to drop, and he stood, shrugging the towel off.

"What's happening here?" I asked—whispered. Though in my head, I totally knew what was happening here. We were having our very own *Ghost* movie pottery wheel moment. Never in my life did I think I'd have a pottery wheel moment.

That was when he took my mouth in a powerful kiss. He moved slowly, worshiping my body. Caress after caress. Not hurried, meandering. He took his time building me up. Years to remove my outer clothing. Millenia for my under-garments. I wanted to return it, but other than mouth kisses, he wouldn't let me do a thing.

My heart felt so full, I feared it might explode. He didn't know I'd fallen for him, but the way he worked my body made me feel like he might have a clue. And he returned it. Right there, on the carpeting separating the living room from the kitchen, Lennon, no other words for it, made love to me.

Forget orgasm mountain. We boarded the orgasm space shuttle, launched into orgasm space, and orbited around the orgasm planet. Our OMS burned hot. The hottest.

How could he make me feel like this? We hadn't been together long enough. I mean, didn't it take time? Less than a month, wasn't that too fast?

No. That was fearful Kami talking again. We'd spent nearly every hour since he'd rescued me in that bar together. So no, not too fast. Other people would call it fast. They might even confuse it with insta-love. But I never claimed to have fallen in love at first sight. Lust at first sight, sure. But not love. Forget that. Forget all of that.

Those other people, they weren't in this relationship with Len and me.

Forget them.

Forget them.

Forget them.

On a deep breath, I started to tell him. Started to but didn't get the chance, because as chance would have it, he beat me to it. "I love you, Kam. I'm in love with you. If it scares you, I'll do anything I have to, to prove it—put you at ease."

I started to laugh.

"Not the response I was hoping for." His voice sounded sad, but he hugged me tightly to him despite my reaction.

"You don't get it. I'm laughing because... well, because I was just about to tell you that I'm in love with you. But you got there first."

"Baby, you just made me the happiest man in the world." He paused and a devilish grin split his lips. "Now, we have a week of no sex to make up for. It'll be a sacrifice, but I need to know, are you with me?"

FIFTEEN

"Where are we going now?" I asked. My girl parts finally got a Lennon reprieve at about 3:30 this morning. Of course, I didn't complain. Len loved me and he showed me in every position he knew. I think he made up a few on the fly.

We'd been driving for about twenty minutes.

That was when he turned to make the drive off the highway. Up ahead of us I could see a tall, unfinished bridge. Tall and unfinished. I got a bad feeling. A booth which looked like a toll booth sat to the driver's side. Len eased to a stop and rolled down his window.

"Welcome to Jump," the girl in the booth said in greeting. "Will you be jumping or observing today?"

"Jumping, naturally." Len winked at her, that flirty, sexy wink that made all the girls' panties wet.

"Up the drive, you'll turn to the left," she said. "Have fun, and be safe."

It wasn't until he started driving again that what he'd said sunk in. "Jumping? What do you mean, jumping? Who's jumping and from where?"

"We are, baby. From that bridge."

My mouth hung open and all I could manage was a few squeaks as he turned the truck to the left and drove into parking lot.

"You still trust me?" he asked.

Deep breath in. Deep breath out. "Yes." Because I did. Even more now.

"You'll be hooked to bungees and fall over water. You'll be perfectly safe. My friend owns this place. You want to leap from an airplane, this is the next step."

Yes, I had to jump from an airplane before we left for the open sea. Crazy Kami wouldn't step foot on that vessel. I nodded my head in defiance of the old me. "Let's do this, then." And I hopped out of the pickup.

My stomach began that nauseous cramping bit when Len sat me down to sign the stack of wavers and consent forms. He signed his no problem. My hand didn't want to write my signature. Mentally, I yelled at my hand, told it we had to do this and to grow up.

My hand called me a series of mean names, tried to tell me I wasn't the boss of it and I needed my head examined. I never had this issue with my hand when I went to jump out of a plane. I wonder if that was because deep down, I knew I wouldn't back out today.

Finally, in sync with my hand, I scribbled my name or initials where appropriate and handed the forms off.

A tall man with a prominent scar cutting through his eyebrow approached us. "Len, buddy. It's been a while." The man had a broad, white smile.

"Sure has," said Len. "I've been busy. Setting sail end of next week."

Then, as if the man had just noticed me, he said, "*Hello. And who might you be?*"

"I'm Kami," I said, holding my hand out to him.

As the man shook it, Len moved in close to press his front to my back. "This is my girlfriend, Jake. She's sailing out with me."

"Kami—*the girl*—the one?"

Len punched Jake in the gut, and it looked pretty hard. Jake made an *oomph* noise and stepped back on one foot.

"Got it," he coughed out. "Nice to meet you, Kami."

What was that about?

"Rude much?" I asked Len.

Len simply shrugged. "Now we have an understanding."

"You couldn't have used your words?"

"For some guys, words aren't enough."

"And Jake is one of those guys?" I asked. Not that I needed an answer. His gut punch pretty well clued me in.

Like at the airplane jump, they had lockers for us to lock our valuables inside. Unlike at the air jump, we didn't need a jumpsuit. One of Jake's assistants helped Len in to a harness while the man—Jake himself—helped me into mine, his hands often getting a little closer to friendly than I was comfortable with.

"Watch your hand now, or watch it dangling broken in a minute," I warned him.

"*Feisty*," he said. "No wonder Len likes you."

"Len loves me. Would you like him to prove it to you?" I turned my head and called, "Hey, Le—"

Jake's hand wrapped around my mouth to muffle my words. "You don't need to do that."

"Oh, but I think I do," I said. Though with his hand over my mouth it sounded more like, "Owe, mut I hink I to." And then I bit him.

Jake howled, shaking his hand out. "Listen, you can't jump if I'm bleeding."

"Fair enough. Hands to yourself, yeah?"

"You're all his," he said as his consent.

From that point on, Jake treated me like any other customer. Harnessed and with helmets on, we walked up to the unfinished bridge, which Jake had turned into his platform for jumping off of.

One end of the thick bungee he hooked to a metal railing with a hook as big as my hand. Then, per his directions, I climbed over the railing to stand on a ledge.

"Right, Kami. Now I want you to bend your knees, spring up and back, understand? You'll be fine. The bungee will stretch and snap you back up a couple of times before you dangle. The second bungee will be used to pull you over to the platform lower down. They'll help you out of your harness."

"Got it."

"You can do this, baby." Len kissed me. "I'll be videoing you the whole way down."

On the count of three (I bent my knees), two (I sprang up and back), one. The air rushed over my face, so loud in my ears. Vaguely, I became aware that I screamed like a gleeful maniac. And I wasn't scared. Not this time. I looked at the river below growing closer as I fell until the bungee couldn't stretch anymore and snapped me back up. I dropped a second time. The bungee snapped me back up a second time, not as high, and I dropped a third and final time.

"*Woo!*" Len screeched. "Good job, Kams. *Woo!*"

I looked up and waved to him and his phone, knowing full well I looked like an idiot in the video. Did I care? Not one single, solitary bit.

Crazy Kami just bungee jumped off an unfinished bridge over a river. "I want to go again," I called back up to him.

"Wait for me. We'll go again together," Len called down.

The assistants pulled me over to the lower platform and I watched Len fall from below him.

I clapped and screamed and clapped some more. When they pulled him in, I didn't even give him the chance to unlatch the hook from the harness before I launched myself at him. Those strong arms wrapped to hold me tight.

"This was amazing," I said. "You're amazing." You couldn't pry the smile off my face with a crowbar.

We climbed the wooden steps back up the side of the cliff to reach the platform again.

"Going again, Jake," Len informed him.

Still smiling, or should I say smiling again, Jake nodded. "So I heard."

This time Len and I jumped off while holding hands.

What a rush. I thought ziplining and rock wall climbing were fun. This just became my new favorite pastime.

After our second jump, new people had shown up, so we let the assistants help us from the harnesses.

"Still feeling good?" Len asked.

"The best." Yeah, okay. So my giddy cheese factor (i.e. How emotionally cheesy I felt at the moment) might have been hitting critical mass, but this was monumental for me. When we reached the lockers, I could hear my phone pinging with notifications before I got the door open.

He'd posted the jump already.

Holy cow, Kami.

That was amazing.

You go, girl!

On and on the messages funneled in. I didn't realize so many people paid attention to me. The irrefutable proof lay on my phone screen.

Thanx, I responded back to one. *It was fun.*

Len's a beast. Best boyfriend in the world. My response to another.

That last I threw in for Brian's sake. Since I knew he'd been keeping track of my adventures. Not that I wanted to make him jealous anymore—because I didn't care if he was. The Brian ship done sailed.

No, I just wanted him to know, in case there was any doubt, that I knew what he'd done, and how Len treated me was how you treated a girlfriend.

"Got another surprise for you," said Len.

"Lead on," I offered.

We drove to an Amazonian restaurant. I didn't know they had a specific cuisine until we walked inside.

"You've got to be joking, right? Please, Len," I begged. "Please tell me you're joking."

"Sorry, baby. Not sorry, and not joking. You can't eat regular food after hitting a milestone like bungee jumping. We go big or we go home."

"Then let's go home."

"No can do." He took my hand, I think more to keep me from escaping than anything, and led me to a table in the center of the small dining room.

It wasn't fancy at all. No table coverings. The black vinyl on the chairs cracked and peeled. A napkin dispenser and salt and pepper shakers sat on each table. When our waitress approached, she spoke to us in Spanish. Lennon answered her as if he spoke Spanish every day of his life.

"*Sí*," she said, then walked over to the kitchen to put in our order.

That word I knew. *Yes.* Score one for Kami.

"What are we getting?" I asked. "How is Amazonian food different?"

"This cuisine comes from a special part of the Amazon. You'll just have to wait."

It wasn't five minutes later the waitress came back with a soda for me and a soda for Len. They used red-and-white striped, wax-covered paper straws. Ten minutes after our drinks, the entrees began to appear. Fried bananas or plantains. Some sort of greens sautéed in oil and garlic. An unleavened bread. And...

I literally had to bite my lip so as to not offend our hosts by screaming. She set a bowl of ants down next. Cooked ants, along with a large serving spoon. Next to the bowl of ants, white grubs. Lastly—I covered my mouth with my hand and swallowed back the bile—a platter of tarantulas. Of the spider variety. The hair had been singed off and they smelled like they'd been sautéed in bacon fat, like the grubs. But there was no way—a spider? Really?

Len thanked her, as did I.

But once she was gone, I laid it out. "I'm not eating that."

"You'll offend them. You have to."

"No, if you'd have told me that you planned to feed me spiders and grubs, I'd have turned you down flat. This is on you, buddy."

"Please, Kam. Just try it. They taste different than you imagine. We're here. Do this"—he wobbled his lip —"for me?"

Fearful Kami would tell him to go to heck. But I wasn't fearful Kami any longer. Crap, I did not want to do this. But I sucked up my reserves. "You first," I ordered.

He scooped up the ants first and dumped a pile on his

plate. Plantains, greens, grubs, a whole spider, and lastly, he tore off a strip of bread. The ants and greens he layered on the bread, which he folded over to make a kind of sandwich. Then he took a big bite.

He chewed.

He swallowed.

He didn't get sick.

Actually, he went back for a second bite right away.

"Okay, I'll try that," I said.

Before I could chicken out, he handed over his last bite. I put the whole thing in my mouth because it wasn't that big. The greens tasted slightly bitter, as greens tended to do. The bread tasted like bread. There was a crunch like eating the crispies from a chocolate covered crunch bar from the ants, and then the oddest sensation. I tasted lemon. Lemon and greens always went together.

"Wow," I said around the mouthful of food. "That's...unexpected."

"Right? Would you like more?"

I shook my head *yes*, so Len piled ants, greens, plantains, and bread on my plate. I hadn't even gotten to the plantains yet.

"Ready to try the grubs yet?" he asked.

"Are you?"

He picked a fat one up and plucked it in his mouth. I watched closely for wincing or cringing as he chewed. He gave no negative responses, so I picked one up, too.

"Here goes nothing," I said, then bit the sucker in half. It didn't squirt like I expected. The insides, having been sautéed in the bacon fat, were solid, and pretty much all I tasted was bacon. I didn't enjoy them—it was a texture thing —as much as the ants, but I didn't hate them either.

Finally, we made it to the big show. The spider he

dropped on my plate. I couldn't watch myself eat it, so I closed my eyes. It crunched, audibly. With my eyes closed, I would have sworn in a court of law that he'd switched out the spider for crab.

That's exactly what it tasted like. Crab.

Upon opening my eyes, I still held a tarantula. Who would've thunk? Tarantulas tasted like crab. Len captured me devouring every bite on camera to post for my followers.

"You have to try this," I said to him, taking another bite without being prodded into it. Pretty much the only thing I didn't go back for was the grubs. I left those to Len.

What does one get to follow up a dinner of insects?

Frozen yogurt.

He took me to his favorite frozen yogurt shop afterward. We built our sundaes and went for a stroll outside. The balmy night made for a wonderful backdrop, with the man whom I loved at my side.

"Can you even believe that things we did today?" I postulated.

"Absolutely. I knew you had it in you, Kam. You're my fearless girl now. Unstoppable."

"You think?"

"What I think is that you're ready."

I shoveled another spoonful of cheesecake frozen yogurt and a fat blackberry into my mouth. "Ready?"

"Jump with me. Tomorrow. I'll be next to you the whole time. What do you say?"

"Seriously, do you really think I'm ready?"

"I've never met a woman readier to take that plunge. C'mon, baby. Say you'll do it."

I thought about it for all of a minute. "Okay, you're right. I'll do it."

For my reward, I got Len kisses. Lots and lots of Len

kisses. Yes, in public. It wasn't like he shoved his tongue down my throat.

That would come later.

SIXTEEN

THE FALL

"I can't do it!" I yelled against the rushing air, making it hard to hear myself, let alone for Len to hear me. The roar rumbled through my entire body, vibrating down to the tips of my booted toes.

"Yes, you can," Len yelled back. "You're fearless now."

"Maybe she can't," Lacy, my former jump instructor, yelled to him.

"She can," Len insisted. "You can, Kam."

We stood in the open doorway, Len and I hooked together fourteen thousand feet up in the sky. He had one hand braced to the top roller and the other to the door pushed open as far as it could go.

How dare she have so little faith in me? Lacy had been the one to dump me as her jump trainee in the first place.

Lennon believed in me.

I looked over my shoulder at Lacy, "You got your camera on?"

"Yes," she hollered back.

Well, then. I turned my neck to kiss Len. "Let's do this."

He leapt from the plane and I closed my eyes. The

wind, I swear, pushed my face flat, rippling the skin around my cheeks. Somehow, he knew I'd closed my eyes.

"Open your eyes, Kami. Baby, you'll regret it, you don't."

What was I doing? He was absolutely right. The biggest fearless moment of my life—*I'd jumped out of an airplane*—and I was missing it. Well, not today. No way. No how. I popped my eyes open. The ground rushed up at me, or I rushed down toward it. Like with the bungee jumping, I squealed out of utter delight. If I'd have been able to clap my hands together and singsong, "*Hercelese, Hercelese,*" I would have.

"Hang on," Len shouted. We'd maybe fallen for sixty seconds tops when he pulled the ripcord and the parachute sprang from his backpack.

We jolted from our freefall, like hitting the brake on a car really hard, when the chute opened fully. Then we drifted down. Len tugged on handles connected to the parachute, which acted like rudders to direct us to the landing zone.

I lifted my feet before we touched down, a skill I remembered but didn't think I'd ever use. Once his feet hit ground and he steadied us, I touched grass. The landing took seconds and Len was so graceful. Of course, he did it for a living, but my Spidey senses told me that Len had that kind of first-time grace that instructors raved about.

Lacy landed just after us. "I can't believe it," she said. "How'd you get her to do it?" That, I was sure, was directed to Len.

"Kam always had it in her." He set about unhooking the parachute, and then me from him so he could turn me around to face him. "I'm so proud of you. So darn proud.

For the rest of your life, you'll have today. You'll know you conquered your fears and jumped out of an airplane."

"Good job, Kami," Lacy said to me. "I'm uploading this footage to the site. I'll send it to you, Len, when I'm done editing."

"Thanks, Lace."

After we gathered up the chute, we walked back to the hangar. Len was busy putting away the gear when he asked, "What do you want to do next?"

"I don't know. Maybe swim with the sharks?"

That got me a huge, boisterous, throw-your-head-back laugh. "I meant today, but I like how you think. That can be arranged—for us to swim with sharks. I got a friend who runs a boat out of Isla Mujeres. He'll totally hook us up."

"What about Iceland?"

"We're still going, destination Iceland for the wedding, remember? After, though, Meredith and Brandon are adventure junkies, so they pretty much do whatever I put on the schedule. And September is the best month to swim with the whale sharks. That'll give us plenty of time. Besides, that side of the world..." He stopped, like to think. "Ever thought about climbing to Machu Picchu?"

"Like the Incan city, Machu Picchu?"

"No, like the burger joint, I'm starved—*yes*, the Incan city."

I unzipped the jumpsuit and stepped out, handing it off as I thought about it. Me at Machu Picchu? "I do like burgers," I answered instead.

"But we can grab burgers before we head home."

We stopped off at a local bar, Bill's, for the best burgers in town. I actually showed Len this place. Bill's was home to the buffalo burger, a thick patty dipped in wing sauce with blue cheese and pickled carrot and celery chips on top. It tasted as good as it sounds. And because we both suffered from a serious fried food weakness we left with an order of fried mushrooms, hand-dipped onion rings, and cheese curds to share.

It was about the time we pulled in to the parking lot to the condo—and a car I didn't recognize had parked in Len's spot, which meant he had to park in visitor's parking because my car was currently seated in his second spot—that I started to regret the choice to carry out instead of eating in.

Not because of the car I didn't recognize, but because of the man sitting on Len's stoop, who presumably drove the unrecognized car. The man I *did* recognize. Absolutely, one hundred percent, recognized.

Brian.

What the hey-hey?

"Kam," Len started. "Would you like to tell me why your ex-douche is on the stoop?"

"I have as much idea as you do." I opened the door to hop out and called over my shoulder, "But I'm going to find out."

Brian stood when he saw me approach. I had my marching feet and my mean face on. He didn't get to do this. Especially not today.

"Hey, Kams, you look great," he said.

I said nothing, opting instead to shoot the evil stink eye. A glare I'd perfected years ago and that was usually effective.

"I saw your video," he continued, undeterred. "Proud of you."

Hmm... stink eye not working. Scowl engaged. "How did you find me?" I asked.

"Internet. It's not hard."

"Great, so... *stalker*. You need to go. Len and I have buffalo burgers to eat and you aren't invited."

"Buffalo burgers? From Bill's?" he asked, oblivious to the mounting tension or choosing to ignore it. "Those are the best."

Was this guy for real? "Aren't you supposed to be in Argentina with New Zealand Kiki?" I asked, exasperated.

"New Zealand Kiki?" he asked back, sort of chuckling.

All his chuckling achieved was to piss me off even further. I placed my hands to my cocked hips. *"Yes, New Zealand Kiki,"* I ground out. "So why are you here?"

"We got back about a week ago. Dierdre texted." Then he turned to address Len. "Man, I thought something was up. Those videos of Kam doing all that stuff I could never talk her into. Who was this supposed superman? So I decided to check you out." I assumed this next bit was for my benefit, as he looked my way when he said it. "It's a good thing I did."

That was when I felt Len press his body to my backside and Brian's face took on a scowl of his own.

"Leave," Len ordered. "You're on private property. Worse than that, you lied to her, man. Cheated on the best woman you'll ever know."

The ugly laugh from Brian didn't leave me feeling too excited about whatever was about to spew from his down-turned mouth. "You wanna talk about liars? Okay, Lennon McCartney. Let's talk about liars."

That sounded ominous. I twisted my head to look between Len and Brian. No, no, no... What could Brian know about Len that I didn't?

"Do you remember your brother's best friend, Kams?"

Slowly, I dipped my head in a half-nod, not wanting to

confirm anything, mostly because I didn't want to hear where this was going.

"What was his name?" Brian asked.

"Harrison."

Brian waved a '*come on*' to keep me talking. "His whole name," he said.

"Harrison... Mc*Cartney*." My shoulders dropped. That was why Len's last name seemed familiar when he gave our reservation. I was such an idiot. In my defense, it wasn't like I used Harrison's last name all the time. He was always just *Harrison* to me. Clearly, I knew it. It just wasn't something I thought about all the time. And it had been several years since I thought of Harrison at all. Okay, I was still an idiot for not putting two and two together, but it never occurred to me. Never.

"Yeah," he replied indignantly. And I never wanted to punch somebody so badly in my life.

Len remained uncharacteristically quiet behind me.

"What was his brother's name?" Brian asked.

"Leo." I answered quickly. I'd never forget that name. The man had practically ruined my life.

"You gonna tell her, or should I?" He directed the question to Len. But then he didn't give Len the chance to speak. "How about *Lennon* 'Leo' McCartney?"

Wait—no. That wasn't possible. I stepped away from Len, off to the side so I had enough space between me and both men.

But I did turn to Len. "Tell him he's wrong. You weren't the one who made threats against my life. Who got me fired from my job... who made me have to move two and a half hours away from my family to start over. *Please*," I begged. "Tell him he's wrong."

"He's not wrong," Len whispered.

At the same time, Brian said, "I looked him up."

This could not be happening. I gripped my hair and pulled the sides. I would not cry... I would not cry... I would not—*shoot*. Those stupid tears began to leak from my eyes.

"You love me, Len," I said. "You told me you love me. How—*why*—how?"

"Don't be dim, Kams," said Brian. "Of course he doesn't love you. This is just some scheme to hurt you again."

"Shut your mouth," Len warned Brian. "You don't know what the hel—*k* you're talking about." Len took a step forward, like he didn't know if he wanted to punch Brian or reach for me.

I took my self out of the equation by turning to run. Yup. I ran, first to the truck to get my purse and the bag with the burgers because lying Len didn't deserve buffalo burgers, and then to my car.

No one could ever accuse me of being a peeler-outer from parking lots. Today I peeled out. My tires squealed and my head hit the ceiling of the car when I hit the street too fast and bounced hard.

Note to self: get shocks and struts checked.

What could've been his motive? Why after all this time would he come at me again? And to get me to do all the things I was afraid to do. It didn't make sense. At all.

I swiped at my eyes. Then I drove to the only place I knew no one would look for me. Two and a half hours in the car, not back to my childhood home. Seeing my parents' disappointed faces when I told them how Len had lied to us all, when I let them know their only daughter had not yet discovered the cure for stupid as she'd been trying these past few years to do—it wasn't something I could deal with now.

Oh, and I angry ate the heck out of those burgers and

fried mushrooms and cheese curds over the course of that drive. Down to the very last bite. Another bad decision. The food sat like a greasy lead weight in the pit of my stomach. But we bought it, I didn't want to waste it. There were starving kids in the world who would've been happy to get my Big Bill's.

Once I reached my fair old city, I turned down a street opposite of the way I'd go to see my family. An old road, bumpy and cracked—what the city called deteriorating—edges. I drove along the chain-link fence until I hit the wrought-iron gate. Ashwood Cemetery.

It had been years since I'd last stepped foot on this sacred ground. The mound of dirt covering my brother had been fresh, no grass. I never felt like I deserved to be here, and anyway, coming back was just too hard. But I needed my brother today.

Funny, the memories of that day, the twists and turns to get to him came to me as if I drove this route twice a week. My parents had picked Ashwood not only for the beauty. Especially in the fall when all the ash trees turn shades of purple, red, yellow, and green. Though, that happened less now since the beetles hit, and not of the British Invasion variety.

The newer, younger trees were a variety called Blue ash and, from what Mom said, just kind of turn a muddy yellow baby poop color. My brother deserved better than baby poop. But my brother rested in a spot very close to my grandparents. So he always had company. I never thought that part mattered. To my mom, it mattered.

I pulled over to the shoulder of the narrow road and turned off the engine. He was maybe twenty headstones away from the road. Being summer, the grass crunched underfoot and the space smelled of dirt and sunshine.

"Evening, Grandma. Grandpa," I said as I passed each headstone. I'd never been close with either of them, seeing as they'd died when I was quite young, which meant I didn't feel the need to converse.

Now when I reached my brother's stone, I stopped and read the words. *Loving Son and Brother. Loyal Friend. Brave Soldier. Hero.* He'd been all that and so much more. His whole short life.

"Hey, bro." Not sure what else to say, I sat down and folded my hands in my lap, staring down at his name. Then I took in a big breath. "I screwed up again. Did you know Harrison's brother, Leo, his first name is actually Lennon?" Then it hit me, Harrison. George Harrison. The Beatles. How could I have not put that together sooner? "And I slept with him. But it gets so much worse. I fell in love with him. Right, you're probably thinking, *'What's so bad about falling in love?'* It's Leo. Well, I mean, I fell in love with him as Len. But Mom had to have told you all the stuff he pulled after you and Harrison died. The man made my life absolutely miserable. And for some reason, he found me and did everything he could to make it not miserable... but I don't know why? What could he be planning?"

The wind picked up to rustle my hair and I kind of imagined that was my brother rumpling the top of my head. I could also hear the hum of a car coming from the other side of the cemetery.

"Brian's the one who told me. Yeah, we broke up because I stopped being fun. Then once I started having fun again, because of Len, he's up in my business again. But, dude, he cheated on me. Brian, not Len. And I thought he was supposed to be in South America celebrating his engagement to the chick he cheated with, but no—there he was on Len's door step. I don't get it. I don't get men.

"So I'm here. I need you to enlighten me. Help me understand what I'm supposed to do because I'm lost. I miss you so darn much. And I'm scared. Sad. Confused. Ugh..." Maybe coming here had been a mistake. I rubbed my hands over my face, then rested them on the crown of my head.

The cemetery grew dark as the night set in. I'd been sitting in that same spot for hours, not once gaining the enlightenment I sought. Though I felt closer to my brother than I had in years, so I couldn't exactly call the trip a waste.

I said *goodbye* to my big brother, stood, and wiped off my bottom, then walked back to my car. There were like fifty thousand text messages on my phone, all from Len.

Kam, baby, I'm so sorry.

Are you alright?

I'm worried.

Call me back, plz.

I should have told you.

He's so sorry? Really?

He should be.

Am I all right?

No.

He's worried?

Good.

Call him back?

Was he kidding?

I drove around for a while, stopped to get a chocolate shake and a large cup of ice water from a fast food joint (my mouth was parched from all the salty food I'd consumed earlier and the expenditure of tears later), and found a hotel for the night.

Sleep, despite how drained my body felt, would not come. The moment my eyes closed, I saw Len's face in my mind and the sadness crept back into my heart. Around

3:30 in the morning, a final text pinged. Of course, from Len.

Can't sleep. Not without you in bed nxt to me.

Stupid, stupid me... In my fuzzy-brained state, I called him. Yup, pressed my finger to his contact and called.

"Kami?" He picked up on the first ring, as if he still held the phone in his hand.

"I can't sleep either. You broke my heart, Len—or should I call you 'Leo.' I don't even know."

"I've got a lot to tell you, baby. Please, I'm begging you to give me the chance. Please hear me out."

Would I hear him out? Not to hear him out would be fearful Kami coming back, right? Afraid to hear his reasons. I didn't have to like his reasons. I didn't have to agree with them, but to remain fearless Kami... Yes. Yes, I would. I sighed heavy enough for him to understand what my sigh was about and shifted on the bed to get comfortable. "I'm on the phone and I can't sleep. Make it count."

SEVENTEEN

"First, what you have to know... Do you remember that night I had just graduated and was coming to the bonfire? Your brother and I, we saw you kiss Harrison."

How could I ever forget that night? I'd made the biggest mistake of my life that night, set everything in motion that night. "Yes," I said. "I remember."

"Har had shown me your picture from Christmas. You had on this ruby-red sweater and a black skirt and tall, black boots. You took my breath away, Kam. Then he told me about all the fun the three of you had together, and I started crushing pretty hard."

"Len."

"No, please let me get this out. When I saw you kiss him, it felt like you'd socked me in the gut with a sledge-hammer. And I was so angry at him... He *knew* I wanted to get to know you, maybe ask you out. Har and I fought, with fists, over you. He and I used to be so close until your brother came into the picture. Then, Harrison tells me that I can't try to date you because it would just be too weird. Kam, all I wanted was for you to get to know me, to see if you couldn't find in me the same things I seemed to pick up on in you."

"He told you not to get to know me?"

"Yeah, baby, he did. Then they went ahead with the plans to join the service."

"No, you're wrong. He joined to get away from me. My brother joined because they were best friends."

"They'd been planning it for close to a year."

"You're lying. My brother would have told me. He would have."

"Listen to me. He didn't tell you because he knew how you'd react. They both really wanted to enlist. But your brother wanted to keep it a secret from you because he said you'd guilt him into not going."

My mind raced in a million different directions. Len could not be telling the truth. No way. No way would my brother have hid wanting to join the military from me. "I'm hanging up now," I said.

"No. Please no—Baby, Kam, I'm telling the truth. I freaked out after Harrison died. I'm not proud, but it happened. I stayed away from you because those were my brother's wishes, and then he up and died on me, leaving me completely alone. And I took it out on you because someone had to hurt more than I did, and you were already dating that douche and like I said, I was really messed up."

"I didn't even *know* you," I said. I balled my fist and punched the pillow because it was too late to scream in frustration.

"Shi-*oot*, I know, it was *a projection*. All of it. It took a lot of therapy to realize I'd been jealous of your brother, your family, for having the relationship with my brother that I didn't any longer."

"You ruined my life," I said in a hard whisper. *Great.* The tears began to form again. *Just fricking great.*

"I'm sorry. You cannot know how sorry I am. As messed up as it sounds, when I harassed you, it meant I was still connected to you which kept me connected to my brother. I still had that last piece of life with Harrison. Then you dropped off the face of the planet and I realized how truly screwed in the head I'd been. So I set out to change things. That's why I moved closer to Grand Rapids, to start over. Become a better me."

He laughed into the phone, but not a *ha-ha* kind of laugh. More the I-can't-believe-how-stupid-I-was kind.

"You know," he said. "I only started calling myself 'Leo' when Har showed me your picture. I thought 'Leo' sounded sexier than 'Len.'" He sounded sad.

"I like Len."

"Yeah, well, I like Kami—a lot. I had no idea you'd moved to my city. But imagine my surprise when you showed up to my jump school. That stupid crush came back despite the fact that you weren't the same you any longer. Seeing your smile—the way it lights up the room, the sound of your laugh... listening in to you and Lacy joke around, getting to join in when I could. I had to be a part of that. There's your whole truth."

"I don't know what to say, Len, to any of it."

"Oh—*wait*," He paused for a moment and I heard him swallow. "Brian and I fought and I sort of gave him a black eye. He said that since you were fun Kami again that he wasn't sure how he felt about the other chick. So I punched him. You can hate me for it, but I don't regret it. Now, *there's* your whole truth."

"Do you even love me or was that a lie?"

"Kam, I'm not even going to dignify that with a response."

I sat up in bed, but that didn't feel like enough. With the phone to my ear, I got out of bed and paced the room. Maybe there was a bar close by. Those—*shoot*, what had I been drinking the night Len had become my boyfriend?— well, I could seriously use one or three of those.

"You still there?" he asked.

"Yes. I need time, though. To process everything."

"How much time? We leave on Friday."

I stopped pacing. "Then I guess until Friday."

His voice dropped low. "It'll be hard, but I won't bother you. If you need me, you call. I hope I see you Friday. I'm leaving the condo by nine. You aren't there before then, I'll assume you aren't coming and I'll leave the key under the door. You can stay as long as you like. But I want you with me..." He paused and pulled in a breath. "Love you."

The phone went dead. He hung up on me.

Well, didn't he just give me a lot to think about? I lay down in bed. I mean, I needed to try for at least a couple hours of sleep. My head hurt. My heart hurt. Breakups sucked and we hadn't even *actually* broken up *yet*. I think we'd call this '*a break*' and it fell on me to decide to make the break permeant or not.

The next morning I woke up—so yes, I'd eventually fallen asleep—showered, and checked out. After grabbing a couple chocolate Danish and a large mocha for breakfast at a local place, I stopped in to a superstore to grab some clothes and sundries, along with some snacks. If I had this week to make my decision about Len, I'd do it visiting places I wanted to go.

My first stop was the beach in Tawas. Sitting in the sun felt wonderful. But sitting in the sun alone, not so much.

He'd have gone swimming with me. *Quit thinking about Len, Kam.*

Since that didn't go as planned, I climbed in my car and hit up Dairy Queen for a frozen treat before I took off farther up north. Instead of traveling I75, I traveled the back roads, taking M-23 north. Up to Alpena and then Cheboygan. Finally arriving back in Mackinaw City.

I avoided the pancake house Len and I had eaten at. Right there, next to the dock, in an on-the-spot decision, I bought a ticket for the ferry to take me over to the island. Once boarded, we didn't take the direct route but detoured to go under the bridge. An amazing sight. Breathtaking, really.

Finally, we docked on the island. Finally, a place without a Len memory attached. Unfortunately, I chose a pizza place, which had incredible pizza, but it wasn't the same as eating it with Len.

Then I took a carriage ride to the butterfly house, where stupidly, I took pictures that I knew he'd just love. I ended up at the fort. That, too, was amazing. But would have been more fun with someone to share the experience with.

One of the hotels actually had a vacancy sign, so my guess, someone had canceled. I went in and snapped that room up. It only cost me three hundred dollars. Yes, that was a hard pill to swallow. But I'd never stayed on the island before.

That night, I went to the haunted house, and then on a walking island ghost tour.

The basements of a few of the taverns were spookier than the cemeteries, and these were Revolutionary-War-era cemeteries. Inside the last tavern we went to, we all got a shock. Of the *supernatural* kind. I wanted so much to call Len and freak the heck out. Instead, I called Dion. He didn't answer. Which, after realizing the time, I understood why he wouldn't. As long as I lived, there'd be no forgetting seeing that case of whiskey move by itself.

At the end of the tour, I walked back to the hotel. The bars still held crowds, but I'd gotten so little sleep last night and made myself so busy today that I decided to stay in and crash. The hotel had yellow siding and white trim. The siding appeared to be tinted green under the blue moonlight and there were bouquets of purple lilacs everywhere.

My room was a floral explosion. Mostly cabbage roses in various colors of pink, red, and orange. Very pretty—so not my decorating style. The bed, though, being on the bed felt like I floated on a cloud.

As I only had the room for one night, and I still had two days 'til Friday, I checked out and took the ferry back to Mackinaw City. Still avoiding the pancake house, I ate at a *different* pancake house, which wasn't quite as good, and got back on the highway.

I traveled down M-31 and made stops in Petoskey and did some window shopping in Charlevoix. Two quaint little towns on Lake Michigan. From Charlevoix, I drove to Traverse City, where I booked a room at a beach resort that I found on my phone from one of those travel booking sites.

At check-in, the hotel had several brochures stacked close to the desk. One of them caught my eye. Wine and chocolate. Traverse City had several vineyards located close by. I thought wine tasting would be fun. But pairing wine and chocolate? *Sign me up.*

I followed my GPS deeper into Michigan wine country, snapping pictures and taking videos along the way. The tour of the vineyard left me breathless from its beauty. The real fun started when they broke out the wine.

One wouldn't think it possible to get drunk off of tiny

plastic Dixie-cup-sized wine samples. Ah, one would most certainly be wrong. I tried every sample they offered. And I couldn't decide if this one Ice Riesling or this Cherry red were my favorite, so I sampled and resampled those several times.

A couple of guys moved closer to me, or it could've been one blurry guy. At this point, I didn't know. He looked like he wanted to talk to me. *Come on.* Men were trouble and if I were going to get into trouble with a guy, I'd pick Len.

Len.

I miss him.

I should call him.

To avoid the confrontation, I pulled my phone from my purse and stood to move to a more private location. I wobbled and almost faceplanted on a different table. Maybe I should have eaten again before drinking all those wines.

Just like the other night, Len answered on the first ring. "Kam, you good?"

"*No—*" I slurred. "I'm a wee bit drunk"—I used my finger and thumb that he couldn't see through the phone to measure out a 'wee bit'—"and I want sex." Then I burped one of those tiny, almost-a-hiccup burps.

He laughed into the receiver. "You want sex... from me?"

"Duh, that's why I'm calling. There're a few guys here who I think might want sex with me, or it might be just one guy. I can't tell. But they're not you."

"Baby, where are you?"

"Traverse City."

"You know it'll take me a few hours to get there. What if you sober up and decide you don't want me after all?"

That was a good question. "Don't be logical when I'm

drunk," I said. "Plus, I have a good answer." My brain sort of froze for several beats.

The dead air hung between us before he prompted, "Kam?"

"*What?*" I startled. "I'm here."

A second laugh. "What's your good answer?"

"Oh, that... yeah, I'm in love with you. So..."

"So you're coming to Iceland with me?"

"Well, I was gonna make you sweat and show up at eight-fifty-nine, like in one of those eighties movies. Then when you thought all hope was lost—*boom!*—I'd be there. But now I'm horny and miss you, and I forgive you because that was a really bad time for the both of us. And I'm horny. Did I say that already?" I shook my head.

The rumble from Len's truck sounded in the background. "Which hotel?"

"The beach resort. But I'm not there. I'm at a vineyard."

"Don't drive. *Shit*—sorry, *shite*. Is there an employee nearby, preferably a woman?"

I scanned the room and found the perky blonde who talked about chocolate and walked over to her. "*Here.*" I shoved the phone in her face. "My boyfriend needs to talk to you."

"Sure," she said to me. "Hello?" To him. Then it was a one-sided conversation because I couldn't hear Len. "Yes, sir. We have a service here at the vineyard." Pause. "Absolutely. I'd be happy to." More pausing. "It's my pleasure. She'll be well taken care of." Then she handed the phone back to me. "He'd like to speak with you again."

"His name is Lennon McCartney," I announced. "Lennon, not Lenin... because his mom loved the Beatles, not the Bolsheviks."

Both the woman and Len laughed at me.

"Go with the lady, okay? She's going to put you in a car to take you back to the hotel. Which room are you in, Kam? Do you know?"

I thought hard as I walked, or, more like stumbled along with the woman who guided me by hanging on to my arm. "*Two-Twelve*," I finally remembered.

"Are you sure? I don't want to freak some poor couple out when I knock on the door."

"Nope. I'm sure. Two-Twelve. That is *defently* where you'll find me."

"*Defently*, Kam? You are so never living this down, baby."

"That's okay. Do I get sex?"

The blonde walking slightly ahead of me turned to look at me. She bit her lip like she was trying not to laugh.

"When you're sober," Len answered. "Yes."

The woman placed me in the backseat of a Lincoln Continental. Black. Nice and roomy. Expensive. I hoped I didn't puke on the leather interior. My head felt spinny, spinish? All I knew was the driver helped me from the car and I sort of wobbled before I found my land legs. Though with a great deal of concentration, I walked in a not-quite-straight line back inside the resort and even made it to the elevator on my own.

There were too many buttons and I couldn't exactly tell which one said two. Luckily, a bellhop carrying luggage stepped in with me just before the doors shut.

"Having trouble?" he asked.

"Point me to two?" I asked.

He pressed it for me and the elevator lifted up to the second floor. The doors opened and he held his hand against the open door so they wouldn't close on me.

"Which room?"

"Two-Twelve," I answered.

"Go left," he said, patting my left arm and pointing to the left.

"Right," I said, and just for fun, I turned right.

"No—" he shouted. And threw his hand out in front of him.

"I was just kidding." I turned around to head left. *Yeesh, some people have no sense of humor.*

After triple-checking I had the correct room, I slid the card through the card reader on the door. When the light blinked green I opened the door and went inside to wait for Len. That was when I got the awesome idea to wait for him naked... because I wanted sex. And Len liked me naked.

So I stripped down completely and must have passed out.

Pound. Pound. Pound. Was that in my head or at the door? *Pound. Pound. Pound.* I opened my eyes. *Pound. Pound. Pound.* Nope. That definitely came from the door. I stood up—my head throbbed—and I wiped the crusted drool from the corner of my mouth.

It felt cold in the room and I realized I was naked.

"Kami?"

I stopped and held my breath, spooked like a deer caught in headlights. That was Len's voice. How—crap. I picked up my phone because I had the distinct suspicion that I'd called him.

Recent calls. Len.

"Just a minute." I called to him and frantically scrambled to find something to put on my body, opting for pulling the comforter from the bed and wrapping myself up in that. Then I opened the door.

"Hi," he said. Oh, man, he looked hot. As in sexy, not temperature.

"Hi," I said back. Then I moved out of the doorway. "Come on in."

Len stepped inside and closed the door behind him. We both walked over to sit on the edge of the bed. "Do you remember calling me?" he asked.

Gah! What was wrong with me? I should still be so angry at him. The things he'd done all those years ago, they were unforgivable, weren't they?

I mean, yeah, he was a bully. Bullies could reform. He'd gone to therapy. So did I take the plunge and forgive him? It seemed drunk Kami already had, otherwise he wouldn't be sitting next to me now.

It *would be* the ultimate gesture of fearlessness.

I brought the comforter up over my head to form my own little Len-less cocoon. I needed to block him out if for nothing else than maintaining my own sanity while I considered my options.

However much time I'd taken, he obviously felt I'd taken enough because he tugged the blanket back down to reveal my face.

"Kam, baby, do you remember calling me?"

Oh, yeah. I forgot he'd asked that.

To be honest or not to be honest?

"I didn't. Then I heard your voice and figured I did." Imagine that, honesty won out.

"Dam-dang it. I was worried this might happen."

"Did you bring ibuprofen?" I asked.

He reached inside his pocket to produce a small, white bottle.

Okay, so I had to admit how glad I was to see him. Neither of us were the same people we had been when our brothers died. Now came the time for even more honesty, only this time, with myself.

Here it goes... I'd forgiven him way back in Tawas. That was my bad. I should've called him then. I should have told him I loved him and that it was water under the bridge. Instead I kept us both suffering needlessly.

Yes, one could officially call me a donkey's butt.

He didn't need to know about that right now.

"Did you bring me anything else?" I asked.

To my surprise, Len opened the door again, bent down, and picked something up. A big white bag that read *Olive Garden* on the front. "I brought you pasta," he said as he closed the door again. "Thought you might be hungry."

Ooh, I smelled cream sauce.

"And?" I asked.

"You said you wanted sex, so I brought my penis."

I sucked in a giddy breath and leapt at him. "Penis *and* Olive Garden? I love you, Lennon McCartney."

EIGHTEEN

Twenty-one months later...

The chopper landed us at basecamp. With the whirring blades above our heads, we had to duck as we disembarked. I carried my backpack, but as usual, Len carried most of our gear. Meredith and Brandon climbed off behind us.

"I can't believe we're actually doing this," I shouted. Because shouting was the only way to be heard until the bird lifted. The heavy wind whipped my hair in my face, even though I had it pulled back and secured with a band.

"Second thoughts?" Len hollered back.

Clear of the helicopter, we stood straight and watched it lift off again. The four of us were greeted by seven others, including two Sherpas, our trek leader, and a medic.

The leader, Kyle, walked over to shake our hands. "Welcome. Get set up. We've got some good stew in the mess tent. Weather forecast is clear for tomorrow, so we'll be heading up first light."

I helped Len set up our tent. He'd obviously done this more times than most and didn't require my help, but he accepted it anyway. The wind still blew in some heavy gusts, but that meant little this far up. We secured the tent into the thick layer of snow and ice with pins two fingers-width thick. Although the sun shined down on my face, we felt very little warmth.

Gear stored, Len and I headed for the mess tent with our metal plates and cups. We found a stew of root vegetables and chunks of yak meat. I'd never eaten yak meat before. Something new to add to the list. They also had this curdled yak's milk cheese that tasted ripe and still had yak hairs in it.

Oh, well. When in Nepal...

Bellies full, we talked for a while with our groupmates. Jan and Taika, a couple from Helsinki, had been married fifteen years and this was their anniversary gift to one another. They had three kids back home and were avid naturalists—which I admit kind of weirded me out because I thought by naturalists, they were talking the nudist variety, but as it turns out what they meant was environmentalists—who farmed their own naturally sustainable, organic food sources. While Byung-joon, a business man from Seoul, tired of the grind, did what Brian had done. Quit his job, sold off his possessions, and made his way here, the first stop on the rest of his life.

I explained for Len and me. "We've been together for almost two years. I gave up my apartment for a job and stayed with Len, but we spent every night together, so I never moved out. We did bring two Cockapoos into our home, too. They stay with our good friends Dion and Henri when we go out of town. We're here because those two"—I pointed to Meredith and Brandon—"like to travel and Meredith wants good hair for her pictures. I'm a hair dresser. Len's an adventure guide."

Brandon spoke for them. Actually, he shrugged and said, "We're rich."

Probably at about 10:00, we hunkered down for the night. The wind had picked up pretty steadily and it rattled the sides of the tent.

"Basecamp nookie?" Len asked, a glint of hopefulness in his eyes.

"Do me, big boy," I teased.

The best part was that with the wind howling so loudly, no one could hear me. And my awesome boyfriend hit all the right places. I sang for the angels.

We woke at first light and packed up our gear. Snow-suits required. Hats, gloves, boots, crampons. Once everyone had finished breakfast, because this was not the kind of hike one started on an empty stomach, our leaders positioned themselves two to the front and two to the rear, and we hiked.

For hours.

The wind picked up and even blew some snow around. We made camp for the night. Each individual or couple was responsible for our own food at the satellite camp. Len and I slept hard. No nookie.

Next morning we packed and started again. Up the mountain. Up. Up. Up. We reached a giant crevasse. If you looked down into it, you couldn't see the bottom. That was how far down it went.

Kyle hooked himself to a rope and scaled the crevasse, then Mandy, the medic, hooked each one of us, one at a time, to the rope, and Kyle helped pull us over to his side. It reminded me of the day Len and I had first done the zipline. Only, one didn't zip across this line. We pulled with our arms while our legs dangled.

Halfway across the giant gap, I looked down and

thought I might pee my pants. But I had Len at my back, cheering me on, giving me the motivation to keep going.

At one point, we got so warm from all the climbing and clear weather, that people started unzipping and/or taking their coats off.

Who would've thunk, sweating in below zero temps? In all seriousness, the idea of it seemed impossible, but there we were or there they were—undressing in this weather. Len and I wore state-of-the-art winter gear that wicked away the sweat and moisture to keep us totally dry. The kind of state-of-the-art winter gear only Meredith and Brandon could afford to pay for. Because they wanted us here, they paid for all of it.

Taika's crampon hit something in the ice and she slipped, sliding backward down the slope. Jan and Len lunged for her, each getting an arm. Taika screamed. I screamed. I thought even Jan screamed. Our leaders doubled back and the ones at the end ran forward to help, but her man and my man had already saved the day. We stopped for a rest after that because that close call ended up way too close for comfort.

It turned out her crampon had hit a shovel from probably the late 1800s or early 1900s.

Every so often, Len pulled his phone out to video our progress, even though he continued to wear that stupid helmet with the camera attached. We posted all the time to social media. And we even ran a travel blog, so our reach went way beyond that of friends and family. My dad loved the blog. He and my mom commented on every update. They loved to show us off to their friends. Yes, *us*. Len and I were a package deal with those two. Especially since my dad had recovered fully from the heart attack and the stent kept his pesky artery unblocked, we surprised them with a trip to Mexico. My parents went swimming with sharks.

At camp three, we stopped on a ledge of the Lhotse wall. At each interval, we had to take time to acclimatize to the elevation so we didn't get elevation sickness. That can kill fast. Like a diver getting the bends. It was all rope climbing once we left camp three.

For our final camp, we hit a compacted snowfield. Solid. Relatively safe, considering we were up on a mountain. But before we reached camp four, we had to climb with the ropes again. At least we stayed to an elevation where supplementary oxygen hadn't become necessary yet.

Plus side.

Once we left camp four, because of how steep and slick the sides were, we used ropes the whole rest of the way up. It got so cold. I didn't remember ever being so cold in my life. Even Len's arms couldn't warm me up.

For weeks and weeks, we worked our way up, trudging through ice and snow, but oh my goodness, nothing could have prepared me for seeing that summit come into view. It reminded me of that first camping trip with Len and we stood at the top of Michigan's highest peak. I didn't think much could compare to the beauty surrounding us there. Being here, I knew how wrong I was.

How very, *very,* wrong I was.

As a group, we hiked our way to the top.

We were literally on top of the world.

As a safety precaution, Kyle instructed us all to don our oxygen masks. Tears filled my eyes. Normally I wasn't a happy crier, and maybe it was as much from relief as anything else, but it could not be helped.

I turned away from the vista spread out *below* us to find Len. I wanted to see his reaction. But I couldn't see him.

Then I felt a tug on my jacket and I looked down. As best he could, Len bent on one knee, his thick glove off one hand so he could hold an open ring box.

Our group surrounded us. They all had their cameras out videoing us instead of the view. I covered my mouth, well, my respirator, with my hand.

"Kami, when we met, you couldn't jump out of a plane. Now not only have you conquered that feat, but you've swum with whale sharks and hiked to Machu Picchu. Navigated a ship through a hurricane. Now you're here at the top of the world. And I'm asking for one more big thing..." He took in a breath. "Conquer marriage with me, baby."

I looked him square in the eye. "No," I stopped for dramatic effect, giving the best acting performance of my life. "I don't think so."

His face dropped. The mood of our group dropped. I threw my head back and full-on belly-laughed.

"Of course I'll marry you, you nut." I had to shout it because the wind thundering across the summit of Mt. Everest boomed in our ears.

Everyone started laughing along with me, except Len, who stood and tore my glove from my hand so he could slide the gorgeous gem on my finger. He pulled up my mask for just a moment so he could kiss me.

BONUS FIRST CHAPTER FROM D.I.E.T. (DATING IN EXTREME TIMES)

THE SHOCK

"Geet!" My boss and admittedly one of my best friends, Dion, called out to me not in greeting, but waving a flat card in his overly zealous hand. "Did you get yours yet?"

Get mine *yet*? I hadn't been home yet to check my mail. Was I supposed to be getting one, whatever it was, he waved around like a lunatic?

Instead of moving to my station, I stopped and waited, suspicious of what was going to come out of his mouth. "That depends... what am I supposed to be on the lookout for?"

"Girl, you really haven't seen? Henri and I are already making plans... I just got off the phone with him after I got off the phone with her and she told me to expect it. I'm so freaking *over the moon*—ten percent off styling products for the rest of the day!"

Ten percent? Wow. He must really be '*over the moon*'.

"That's great, but *what* is *it*?"

"Our Kami is getting married!" he shouted and danced around the salon. "Married... Married..." he continued to singsong as he made his way over to my station to hand me his invitation.

"It's an invitation to a reception, not a wedding," I said, looking over the front and back to see if I'd missed any pertinent information. Nope. What it said on the front of the card was all that was there.

"*I know!*" Dion shouted. But right as I was about to attempt to calm him down a bit in order to find out what exactly got him this excited, the front bell chimed and we both turned to see two of our regular clients walk in.

I led my first client into the back room. We were a full-service spa. Dion did hair. The best hair in the state of Michigan now that Kami was off galivanting all over the world with her now fiancé. It took us a while to fill her shoes but after a month of nonstop interviews, we hired on two new stylists. Once word got out that Kami was snatched up by *the* Meredith Lowenstein, every woman of means or with a high balance credit card sought us out. We could've done with four new stylists but Dion wanted to keep the waiting list going because in the rich set, a waiting list obviously meant the best.

I, however, held the privilege of being Affinity's only in-house masseuse. Mrs. Danvers needed my 'magic hands' because her divorce was turning nasty now that Mr. Danvers found out about the pool boy and Mrs. Danvers found out about the pool boy, too. Then there was Ms. Jacqueline, who's *Booboo Pookie* was sick at the vet and then there were the Bellamy twins who made their money off of nudie pics on the internet, in calendars and even a coffee table book. Their muscles got tense from holding those poses all day. I say, good for them. If I looked like them, I'd show it off, too.

The never-ending parade of clients coming through the

door kept me from getting to the bottom of why Dion got so overly excited about an invitation to a reception. And when I finally handed off my last client of the day, Dion was arm-deep in product to put the finishing touches on a glamorous hairstyle.

After clocking out, I bundled up in my Sherpa gear to face another freezing night of polar vortex insanity complete with snowdrifts taller than my Jeep and potholes deep enough to be mistaken for sinkholes—perfect for ruining the alignment on a car—taking off to run some errands and grab dinner. I'd been out of work for maybe fifteen minutes when my phone rang while I was waiting in the drive thru of Happy Burger. Kami's name lit up the screen.

"*Kams!*" I answered.

"Geet. I'm so glad I got you. How've you been?" she asked, and I'd swear she was bouncing on the other end of the phone, waiting to tell me her news.

"Fine. Clearly not as fine as you. Dion got his invite today."

"Yeah—you have one, too. But I needed to talk to you. I got Dion this morning before he left for work," she said.

"What's up?"

"Len and I decided we want to get married at Albatross Monument on Cape Horn Island, Chile. We're having a reception closer to home for people who can't make it, but Geet... I'm really hoping that you aren't one of those. We want you there with us. Dion, Henri, you. The Lowensteins and a couple of Len's friends. Please, I can't get married without you there."

"I—*Cape Horn?*" I kind of, okay, I totally screeched.

"Please," she begged again. "If it's the cost—"

"That's not it." And it wasn't. I could afford the trip. I'd been saving for a major trip for the past couple of years. But a major trip required a travel buddy because who wanted to globe trek alone? It'd been a couple of years since I even went out on a date and Kami, until she met Len, wouldn't leave the city unless she headed home to see her parents.

"Then what is it?"

I decided to be honest, because if you couldn't be honest with your best friend... "Do you realize how many steps there are to get to Albatross Monument?" I'd heard of that; it was located on the southern-most scrape of land before you reached Antarctica. *Antarctica.*

"Geet, it's not that many steps."

"Says the beauty queen with the body of a fitness model who climbed to the summit of Mt. Everest. You do remember what I told you my nickname in school was? *Doughy.* They called me doughy and they called it for a reason."

She giggled but ignored that. "Got engaged on the summit of Mt. Everest," she corrected me and I couldn't help it, my mouth dropped open.

"He purposed at the summit of Mt. Everest? Shoot Kams—I think you found the one perfect straight man in the world."

"He's definitely a keeper, but I'm sure he's not the only one... and you're deflecting."

I pulled up a search engine on my phone to look up Cape Horn Island. "It says on the website that there are only seven cruise ships capable of disembarking at Cape Horn Island and Albatross Monument—a monument dedicated to the *thousands* of sailors who died on a voyage through tides so hazardous, even some modern ships aren't able to maneuver close enough to make land, btw—and once on shore, you're met with *one hundred sixty-two* ocean-sprayed steps, but that's not even the worst part. Oh no... that comes up when the stairs level off to a slippery, wooden path that leads you through a tundra of relentless drizzly-misty squalls, strong enough to blast you off into the frigid, soggy land on either side."

"Okay... but you said it yourself, it's only a hundred and sixty-two steps. You can handle that," she said, and I hoped she picked up on *the hand* I mentally put up. "Please, Geet," she softly spoke. "I need you."

Crap. Kami was basically my sister from another mister. I wanted to be there for her. God help me... I sighed and said defeatedly, "Yeah, whenever it is, I'll be there."

She squealed. Squealed so loud I had to mute her for a second. When I unmuted her she was already talking again. "...won't be sorry. This is the best news, *the best*." Then she stopped talking to me to shout, "Len, she's coming."

Despite my apprehension, making one of my best friends this happy was worth whatever I had to do to be able to tackle Cape Horn.

"I have to go now, Geet. We're getting ready to make land."

"Wait—when is it?" I asked.

"Six weeks. February fourteenth." Now if she was here, standing in front of me, I'd give her crap over picking a cringeworthy valentine wedding, but was she crazy?

"You want us to meet at the bottom of the world in *February*? You want us to die?" I yelled.

"Girl, it's summer down here. You think I'd do that to you?"

"*Oh*— I knew that."

"Yeah you did," she said, laughing at me. Jeeze, I missed her. "Summer doesn't necessarily mean warm, though. I'll send the itinerary... but now I really have to go. Love ya, Geet. Can't wait to see you."

"Samesies, babe. Bye." The moment she hung up my heart sank. Her life was moving at warp speed and I loved my job, loved working with Dion, but I wasn't getting any younger. Only five more years until I hit the big 3-0, and everybody knew it was all downhill after the big 3-0.

The car in front of me moved up a spot which allowed me to take my turn at the speaker, rolling down my window to the gust of super chilled air. *"Go ahead with your order when you're ready,"* the Happy Burger worker said.

"Yeah, I'll have the number thirteen double olive super burger with cheese. Medium fry, but can I upsize to a large mocha?"

"You can do that. Does everything look correct on the screen?"

"Absolutely," I chirped.

She gave me my total and I moved up to the window to get my food. On the way home I passed a giant billboard. Super Fitness. The Jerk-free Gym.

Right... jerk-free. I shook my head at the stupid advertisement and clicked my blinker to turn into my complex. Home again, home again... jiggity-jog.

The snow started falling again hot and heavy, well technically cold and heavy, but that's not the saying now is it? It started falling about two miles back and at this rate we were destined to be snowed in completely by roughly midnight. Good thing I went grocery shopping yesterday just in case the snowpocalypse kept me from venturing out my front door tomorrow.

With my arm raised to shield my face, my food bag and I braved the wind whipping gale-force at us, attempting to push me backward one step for every two that I took until the brick building blocked me enough to get my key in the front door.

I hung my keys up on the hook next to the door, looped my purse around my neck and held my mocha by biting down on the lip of the plastic lid in order to shrug out of my coat. I switched the bag between hands to slip my arms out, then hung the coat up on the hook meant for keys. The hard plastic bowed under the weight of the heavy material. My guess, I had probably three more times of hanging my coat there before the whole hook came down.

It took several tries to toe off each clunky, ugly-yet-utilitarian boot. They might have been ugly but they were warm, lined with faux wool. Purse still around my neck, I grabbed the mocha and trudged into the living room, setting the bag and cup down on the coffee table.

Before sitting down, I walked into my bedroom to change into my warmest pajamas. An Eeyore onesie that Dion and Henri got me for Christmas. I loved it, snugglier than anything I'd ever worn. It even had an Eeyore hood and tail to swish.

Now my sofa and dinner called to me. I walked out of my room, plopped down on my sofa, pulled the throw from the back to drape over me, tucked my legs up underneath me and unbagged my burger and fries. But before getting down to the business of eating, I used the remote to flick on the TV, clicked on 'continue watching' Homicide Hunter and flipped open my laptop, powering it up.

If Kami expected me to trek to the top of Albatross Monument to see her say her "I do" then I needed to know exactly, down to the letter, what was expected of me. Chile. Of all the places I could've imagined popping my international travel cherry, Chile would not have topped that list. Yet here I was, listening to Joe Kenda narrate his old cases while researching hotels.

Oh, they had a four star with unbelievable views. An infinity pool that looked like it dropped off into the ocean and a spa. *That would be a change,* I snickered to myself. But most of the tourist attractions involved some form of torture—what I meant was climbing. Cliffs, steps, if they could use it to steal the breath from my lungs, it appeared they made it available. Joy.

I picked up my olive burger and took a big bite, chewing on the meat and my problem some more. As I swallowed, I realized the enormity of my problem. Len, Kami, the Lowensteins and the like would reach the top while I remained stuck no higher than the tenth step, clutching my chest and heaving my dying breaths.

Oh god, oh god, oh god... I had to get out of this trip, but how? I promised Kam. If I turned her down now, she'd be devastated. I couldn't live with myself if I ruined my BFF's wedding. I tossed my partially eaten burger back down on the wrapper, having lost my appetite. This was going to be a complete and utter disaster.

Right. I bookmarked the hotel page just in case I ended up needing it, then opened up my Facebook to distract me while I figured out a way to beg off this trip. And wouldn't you know it, one story down there was an ad for Super Fitness—The Jerk-Free Gym. What were they advertising? Not any ordinary membership, oh no, no, no... A six-week bootcamp. Six weeks? What were the odds? Big Brother had to be listening in to know I needed to shape up in six weeks if I had any chance of not dying during my girl's wedding.

Guess there was no begging off tonight. Instead, I

clicked on the link. Filled out the form and used my credit card to pay for it.

And I still wasn't hungry, but ate my burger and fries anyway knowing that I just signed up for fast food jail.

I had a feeling I was going to regret this decision.

Click the link to see how the rest of the story goes: D.I.E.T. (Did I Eat That?)

SEE HOW BRIGEETA'S STORY GOES IN:

D.I.E.T. (Dating in Extreme Times)

Liked what you've read? Consider leaving a **review** here.

If you'd like to keep up on all my new releases, giveaways and other fun stuff, join my **newsletter** here.

D.I.E.T. (Dating in Extreme Times)

Why settle for a pickle tickle when it's more fun to play hide the salami?

When Brigeeta—or Geet, as her friends call her—gets an invitation to her bestie's wedding, she couldn't be happier... until she finds out the location. Of course Kami and Len couldn't rent a beachfront villa for their special day. They needed something unique... like a hike up seventy-bajillion steps to a monument Geet got lightheaded even thinking about. Worse yet, not one brochure mentioned any kind of elevator to the peak.

To lessen the odds of her needing a defibrillator mid-climb, she hires a personal trainer to help her get in shape. But not just any trainer. This smokin' hottie might make a good plus one for the nuptials. Unfortunately, flirting proves impossible when he pairs her with Sinjin—a highly attractive workaholic—to keep them both motivated.

With six weeks to get fit, can Brigeeta make the trek to her best friend's wedding with her crush on her arm? Or will she, and her hopes, melt in a heap on the gym floor?

MORE BY SARAH ZOLTON ARTHUR

Adventures in Love Series

Skydiving, Skinny-Dipping & Other Ways to Enjoy Your Fake Boyfriend

D.I.E.T. (Dating in Extreme Times)

WTF Are You Thinking?

Holiday Bites (A Lake Shores, MI World)

Baby, It's Cold Outside (Book One by Sarah Zolton Arthur)

All I Want (Book Two by Heather Young-Nichols)

Always Be My Baby (Book Three by Sarah Zolton Arthur)

All of Me (Book Four by Heather Young-Nichols)

Standalones

Summer of the Boy

The Significance of Moving On

Audio

Summer of the Boy

Skydiving, Skinny-Dipping & Other Ways to Enjoy Your Fake Boyfriend

Flight: The Roc Warriors

YA Titles

The Princes of Stone and Steel

ABOUT THE AUTHOR

Sarah spends her days embracing the weirdly wonderful parts of life with her two kooky sons while pretending to be a responsible adult. And there is plenty of the weird and wonderful to go around with her older son being autistic. She resides in Michigan, where the winters bring cold, and the summers bring construction. The roads might have potholes, but the beaches are amazing. And above all else, she lives by these rules. Call them Sarah's life edicts: In Sarah's world all books have kissing and end in some form of HEA. Because really, what more do you need in life?

ACKNOWLEDGMENTS

Thank you to *you*, my wonderful readers, who followed along as Kami found her mojo. Thank you to my boys. You are the best apple and waterfowl a mom could ask for. I am so glad to see the butt-crack of this year, but as long as we continue have each other's backs, we'll always make it through. Here's to a better 2019! And thank you to all coffee everywhere. Whether instant or brewed, vanilla or mocha, iced, frappéd or even hot, my life would be less tasty without you. And without you, these stories would never get written. I am so serious on this point.